In Praise of HONEY

In Praise of HONEY

Honey for Health, Beauty, & Cookery:
Recipes & Traditions

JANE CHARLTON AND
JANE NEWDICK

Boyne Valley Honey Company

PUBLISHED BY THE BOYNE VALLEY HONEY COMPANY
MELL, DROGHEDA, CO. LOUTH, IRELAND

A QUARTO BOOK

Published by
The Boyne Valley Honey Company
Mell, Drogheda,
Co. Louth, Ireland

Copyright © 1995 Quarto Publishing plc
All rights reserved. No part of this publication may be reproduced,
stored in a retrieval system or transmitted in any form or by any means,
electronic, mechanical, photocopying, recording or otherwise, without
the permission of the copyright holder.

ISBN 1–86155–559–8

This book was designed and produced by
Quarto Publishing plc
The Old Brewery
6 Blundell Street
London N7 9BH

Art Director: Moira Clinch
Design: Design Revolution
Senior Art Editor: Liz Brown
Copy Editors: Jackie Matthews and Fiona Hunter
Home Economist: Jane Charlton
Picture Researcher: Jo Carlill
Picture Manager: Giulia Hetherington
Senior Editor: Sian Parkhouse
Editorial Director: Mark Dartford
Photographer: David Sherwin
Illustrators: Fred Van Deelen, Elizabeth Dowel

Typeset in Great Britain by Central Southern Typesetters, Eastbourne
Manufactured in Hong Kong by Regent Publishing Services Ltd
Printed in China by Leefung-Asco Printers Ltd

Contents

6 • Introduction

8 • The Story of the Bee

10 • Bees and their Beehives

16 • From the Hive to the Honey Pot

20 • The Story of Honey

26 • Health and Beauty

36 • A World of Honey

41 • First Courses

56 • Main Courses

74 • Vegetables

90 • Desserts

108 • Cakes and Biscuits

126 • Index

128 • Acknowledgements

INTRODUCTION

Honey has been sought after for centuries. In the past a taste of this amber elixir could placate the gods, arouse feelings of love and inspire great cooks. And the unique flavour of this sweet substance still guarantees it a place in the affections and store cupboards of people today.

Aristotle, one of the earliest believers in honey's efficacy

Honey has inspired many fascinating legends; stories of its magical powers have been passed down through history. People of ancient civilisations realised the value of honey and came up with innovative ways to use it, both as a foodstuff and in other, more esoteric, ways. Pharaohs were sent off to their eternal journey to the after-life with pots of honey, and the enterprising Egyptians also discovered that honey was an excellent medium for embalming their dead.

Great philosophers and physicians, such as Aristotle and Hippocrates were fascinated by the industrious bees. They captured them in hives, studying their complex communities and harvesting the honey for their own consumption.

Astutely recognising both honey's healing power and therapeutic qualities, the Greeks and Romans soon transported the pot of honey from the table to the physician's surgery. Many of the remedies they devised are still used to promote health, vitality and long life today – using their recipes we can make them.

Honey was also seized upon for its cosmetic applications. Legendary beauties such as Cleopatra and Madame Du Barry are among the countless women through the centuries who have included honey in beauty preparations for its purifying and enhancing qualities and modern women can still benefit from it, both in commercial creams and home-made treatments.

Of course, these potions and lotions would

Spiced bread, flavoured with honey.

Beekeeping has an old and venerable tradition, as is demonstrated in this fifteenth-century manuscript.

not exist without the resourceful bee, travelling from blossom to blossom collecting nectar from different flowers and turning it into the treasured golden substance by a process akin to alchemy. We have harnessed this magical skill through beekeeping, and we can now choose from countless varieties of honey from all over the world. Each has its own distinctive flavour and scent: discover reosemary honey from the Mediterranean, eucalyptus honey from Australia, tupelo honey from the United States and lavender honey from France.

We all relish the tastes of honey can bring to everyday foods – toast and honey, for example is a staple from childhood. But historical recipes divulge some more unusual combinations. The famous gourmet Apicius created a whole banquet from dishes prepared with honey.

While we may not find his more exotic recipes very appetising, such as honey-baked tortoise or peacock in honey sauce, we can be inspired by his inventiveness. Honey adds a certain richness of both colour and taste to a variety of foods, both savoury and sweet – simple snacks for any time of the day, honeyed meats and poultry, luscious desserts, scrumptious cakes and tempting drinks.

With such diverse uses it is not surprising that honey is as popular as ever, and many more people are discovering why it was indispensable to ancient civilisations. Honey today is appreciated as an unadulterated, natural product, less processed than any other sweetening agent, and with fewer calories. It is now a major commodity, with a total of nearly a million tons produced worldwide every year.

The honey bee has long been associated with health and well being, so it is easy to see why the organisers of the International Health Exhibition in 1884 should have chosen it as their symbol.

A traditional wooden honey drizzle, used to pour thin streams of honey.

This lid from a jar of blended honey carries the trademark bear of The Bear Honey Company, an animal long associated with honey.

THE STORY OF THE BEE

REMAINS OF PRIMITIVE BEE-LIKE INSECTS HAVE BEEN FOUND ENCAPSULATED IN BALTIC AMBER FROM THE EOCENE PERIOD, SOME 50 MILLION YEARS AGO. THEY SLOWLY EVOLVED INTO THE CREATURES WE KNOW TODAY AS HONEY BEES.

A fifteenth century illustration of a bee from a manuscript with text around it. Very little attempt has been made to draw the insect in an anatomically correct way but the little image of the bee makes a strong and colourful motif.

The domestic honey bee we have today belongs to the race *apis mellifera*. Linnaeus classified it as *mellifera* (honey bearing), then changed it to *mellifica* (honey making) after discovering that the insects made honey in the hive, rather than collecting it. Today there are four species of *apis* in the world, which all build wax combs and store a surplus of nectar and pollen. Before man introduced the domestic bee to different countries, *apis mellifera* was found only in Europe and Africa and there were no honey bee species native to North and South America, New Zealand, Australia, New Guinea or the South Pacific islands.

In effect, there is a class structure of bees with each one having a specific purpose within the colony. The size of a colony of bees can vary enormously but on average at peak population periods, a hive or nest may contain 30,000 to 40,000 worker bees, one queen, and 500 to 1,000 drones. In winter in temperate climates this figure will be reduced to a queen and about 500 to 12,000 workers.

The queen is the matriarch of the colony and she will live for three to four years. Generally, there is only one breeding queen in a hive. She begins life by being reared in a special queen cell in the wax comb, hatching from an egg laid by the previous queen, who will be replaced by her. She is fed by worker bees on a diet of royal jelly and carefully nurtured, licked clean and generally pampered until in sixteen days she is fully grown. Several queens may be raised at the same time, but most will be stung to death.

THE MATING GAME

The queen will mate with the male drone bees. After mating, the queen should have five million sperm stored so that she can begin laying eggs in the brood nest. She will continue to do so through the spring and summer and right up to the winter, when she stops, before resuming again the following spring. She lays fertilized eggs which will become workers in some cells and in other, larger cells she lays unfertilized eggs which will become the male drones.

A foraging honey bee with full pollen sacs working amongst apple blossom in an orchard in late spring. Tree blossoms make up a large part of the plants visited by worker bees.

The female workers in a hive do everything required to keep the colony functioning. In busy times of year, such as the height of summer, they may live for only six weeks. Once hatched, the new workers will be given a sequence of work starting with cleaning and caring for the nursery quarters, then feeding the larvae. At six to ten days old, they will take their first flights outside. Next they start to secrete wax and build new wax cells, then move on to receiving and storing the nectar. At two to three weeks old they progress to entrance guarding and fanning their wings to keep the hive cool and clearing away debris. Only then do they begin to fly from the hive to collect nectar, pollen and propolis, a glue-like substance taken from sticky buds and leaves.

Busy bees

Foraging is what really exhausts the worker bee, taking her up to 5 kilometres from the hive at a time. The bee will suck nectar from deep inside the flower and store it in her honey sac, picking up pollen as she moves amongst the flowers and storing this on her back pair of legs. The journey back to the hive is by the shortest and quickest route (hence the term "making a beeline for.") and once home, the nectar and pollen are taken by another worker or put by her into cells. It takes between 20,000 and 100,000 journeys to bring a litre of nectar back to the hive.

One fascinating aspect of the worker bee's life which has been studied carefully over the years is the means of communication between the bees by means of "dance". For example, at the beginning of the year when the first workers go off searching for nectar, they need to

Australian worker bees and their queen on a section of comb in a hive used for pollen storage.

let the other workers know when they have found it. This is done by performing several different and distinct dances which describe just where the nectar source is and how far away it is. In the 1920s the Bavarian bee expert Professor Karl Ritter von Frisch isolated and identified some of these, which have come to be known as the Round dance, the Wagtail dance and the Sickle dance.

The drones

Virgil described the drones in a hive as "that pack of shirkers" whose main purpose is to mate with the queen. The drone is larger than a female worker, weighing about the same as a queen and with distinctive large compound eyes meeting on the top of the head. Probably only a very few of the hundred males will mate with the queen and at the end of the summer the surplus drones are chased from the hive and harassed until they fly away. Unable to forage for themselves, they soon die of starvation.

The Queen

The queen's body is elongated and her wings extend only part of the way back over her abdomen. Her legs are long with no pollen collecting sacs and her sting is curved.

The Drone

The drone weighs about the same as a queen and has large wings which cover the blunt abdomen. The thorax is quite square and the large compound eyes almost meet.

The Worker

The worker is half the weight of a drone or queen with a hairy body and straight sting. The wings almost cover the abdomen and the legs have pollen collecting apparatus on them.

BEES AND THEIR BEEHIVES

SINCE HUMANS FIRST TOOK BEES FROM THE WILD AND BEGAN BEEKEEPING, HIVE DESIGN HAS EVOLVED DIFFERENTLY ALL OVER THE WORLD.

An elaborate garden design from the 1820s shows how beekeeping fitted into what was becoming a more formal landscape style. Siting the bee shelter by the pool fulfilled two functions: it complemented the overall design and also made it easy to get to the hives.

Before people learned how to keep bees in artificial hives, honey was collected from the wild, often destroying the bees and their nests in the process. The honey bee's natural habitat of a hollow tree was sometimes removed to a settlement by sawing it into a portable size and setting it up as the first kind of domestic beehive. Even then, the bees were generally sacrificed for the honey. The early Egyptians learned how to breed bees in artificial nests or hives made from interwoven twigs and reeds and baked mud. These were shaped like long cylinders and stacked together horizontally with the gaps between them filled with clay. Both the Greeks and Romans used cylindrical hives, made not only from clay but many different materials such as woven wattle, dung, cork bark, wood or logs. Horizontal hives are still used in many less-developed areas of the world today, such as parts of Africa and South America.

THE ALVEARY

The first vertical hives date back to between 100 and 500 AD. The problem with keeping bees in this way was how to extract the honeycomb which was not as simple as removing it from horizontal hives. The usual method was to destroy the bees with sulphur fumes, or by drowning, to get at the comb, leaving just a few colonies to overwinter. The earliest types of hive were made from woven wicker and the remains of one of these have been dated at around AD 200. This simple kind of hive, sometimes known as an "alveary", was conical in shape and made from woven willow or hazel, like a tall pointed upturned basket. The structure was covered both inside and out in cloam (a soft daub made from lime and animal dung which hardened into a waterproof coating, keeping the bees safe and dry inside). A "hackle" or bunch of straw, was pushed over the top of the hive to divert the rain from the sides. Examples of this type of hive were still being used up to 1885.

THE STRAW SKEP

Straw "skeps" were made possibly as early as the beginning of the Christian era in parts of western Europe, and then became widespread throughout the whole of the continent. The origin of their name is puzzling. Some scholars argue that it comes from the Norse word *skeppa*, meaning a container or measure for grain, but it is known that the word skep did not come into common use until about the sixteenth century. In Britain they were still being used up to the nineteenth century, even alongside modern wooden hives, and they are still used today by some beekeepers to collect swarms. The advantages of the straw skep were that the materials were cheap, and few tools were needed to make it. Straw was the commonest material, but in areas where it was scarce reed might be used, or – in uplands with little arable land – purple moor grass. The straw was pushed through a hollow bone or cow's horn to form

A Mr Saul wrote to the Mechanics Magazine in 1829 with this design for his Improved bee-house. It was designed so that the house could be turned so that the entrance was always away from the wind (which must have confused the bees no end) hence the wind vane on top. It also had a device for measuring the weight of the hive and therefore the honey. Inside was a straw hive but the outer construction would appear to be aimed at pleasing bishops or priests rather than mechanics.

The thick cob walls of this Devonshire house are deep enough to have a couple of boles let into them to house bee skeps, although placed where they are reaching them must have been difficult.

Bees and their Beehives

This elegant hive on a pole comes from a period, probably the early nineteenth century, when all kinds of experimental hive shapes were being developed.

tight rolls, which were then coiled spirally and neatly bound together with strong lengths of bramble stem. Skeps evolved and changed shape over the years, becoming flatter rather than conical so that several could be stacked together. Their main disadvantage was that the straw could rot in a wet season, which meant providing some kind of additional shelter.

Bee boles and houses

A "bee bole" was a niche, or alcove, in a house or garden wall where straw skeps could be kept out of the worst weather. In their most primitive form, the boles were often no more than spaces left in a dry stone wall, but in grander gardens and estates they were often built with care and attention to detail. At Packwood House in Warwickshire, England, the garden wall has a series of 30 bee boles let into it. Boles were most common in England and Ireland where they were extensively used in the seventeenth and eighteenth centuries. In hotter countries such as Spain and North Africa, bee walls – stacks of horizontal hives kept permanently in a long wall – were more common. In Germany, bee houses were used to keep multiple colonies of bees together. These were sometimes very elaborate permanent buildings made of wood or stone, with the hives facing outwards in all directions and room inside for the beekeeper to work and get at the hives. This type of bee house spread to eastern Europe, where Austria, Poland, Bohemia and Slovakia all had fine examples of these buildings. A few grand

A traditional bell shaped straw skep from the 1840s.

Wildman's storeyed straw beehive with wooden spars at the top on which the bees could build the comb.

A Grecian or Candiote straw hive with wooden spars for the comb.

country houses in England had specially made bee houses, often in a style of architecture to complement or match the main house itself. Though practical, they were also important as part of the overall design of the garden and the environs of the house.

Modern hives

As beekeeping developed, it became clear that it was no longer acceptable to destroy colonies to get honey or to rob skeps of all the comb, so that the bees starved during the winter. Experiments were carried out to try to make suitable hives which protected the bees and simplified the removal process. By the mid seventeenth century, skeps were "storified", or stacked together, meaning that a box of combs could be removed without killing the colony. Various systems were devised to separate the bees when necessary and to isolate the honeycomb for removal. Professional and amateur beekeepers experimented during the latter half of the eighteenth century and the

From this colony of bees in a hollow tree it is easy to see how the bees construct their comb without human interference. The bees simply fill the available space, and so the wax structure is quite free-form.

This is an Indian pot hive made from earthenware and propped horizontally in the crook of some tree branches. This style of hive was common throughout the ancient world and is still used today.

This is a replica of the earliest kind of wattle and daub hive or alveary. The willow twigs are not totally covered so it is possible to see how they are woven. The whole design has a pleasing almost organic form.

Two styles of nineteenth-century wooden beehives, one simple and the other quite grand, and a traditional straw skep on a stand and with a straw cover.

A female beekeeper works in her apiary of wooden hives in Lismore, Ireland in 1890. She is smoking one hive with bellows and seems prepared to collect some honey with a bowl and spoon.

first half of the nineteenth, and the concept of removable frames became established. These frames could be built upon by the bee and easily removed, but the problem of the bees building between the frames and gluing them together remained unsolved.

The real breakthrough came in 1851, when the Reverend Lorenzo Lorraine Langstroth from Pennsylvania discovered "bee space". This was the space needed between the parts of a hive which was too big for the bee to fill with comb, but left enough room for the insects to move about freely. The Langstroth hive has been the model for most subsequent hives with the WBC, modern Langstroth, and "National Hive Design" all based on the same principal. In 1857, a German named Mehring had the brilliant idea of making sheets of beeswax,

A print published in London in 1851 shows an example of Pettitt's Temple beehive. On the left it is closed and on the right we can see A the feeding drawer, B the brood hive and C two glass hives to be added when B is nearly full of comb.

Examples of eighteenth century hives from Hungary carved from tree trunks and based on the most primitive forms of early hives.

imprinted with the hexagonal cell shape, which were fitted into the frames ready for the bees to build outwards. These sheets of wax are known as foundation and are familiar to many of us as the material used for rolled beeswax candles. At roughly the same time, Abbé Collin in France invented the queen excluder – a sheet of perforated metal used in the hive to keep the queen in the nursery quarters and from laying in the upper chambers of the hive. The workers can move through it and deposit nectar above the queen and then frames full of honey can be removed without disturbing the bees.

Barcs

For centuries, in densely forested parts of eastern Europe, people kept bees in "barcs", or hollowed-out trees. This method was still used up to the 1930s and it made good sense in these areas where trees were the bees' natural habitat. Beekeepers selected old, wide-girthed trees and made one or more cavities, usually about 3 metres from the ground but sometimes up to 20 metres above. A special board was fixed at the entrance to the barc and a log was left to swing in front of the cavity to deter bears from robbing the nest. Honey was harvested once a year, after the honey flow had finished.

A straw hive in France, dating from the 1890s or early 1900s, with an extra top knot to protect it from the sun and a tile to keep the rain out.

In former Yugoslavia elaborate bee houses were very common holding several colonies at a time. This is a hive on a smaller scale in the bee museum at Radorljica but designed as a miniature house, though the complicated decoration makes it hard to see how it worked as a hive for bees.

Experiments have been done to find which colour is best for a beehive. Traditionally they were often painted white but pastel colours such as pale sky blue seem effective for the bee to locate its base easily.

A quite extraordinary wooden beehive made in the shape of a man with the entrance for the bees above his belt and between his legs. It is in a bee museum in Croatia.

From The Hive to The Honey Pot

Beekeepers have always been seen as somewhat special people and held in great respect, particularly by those who know little about bees and see them only as a terrifying, stinging mass. In ancient times beekeepers were revered and held in high esteem, their knowledge and patience considered important and even profound. Luckily for all of us who love honey, beekeeping is still alive and well.

There is no doubt that the first steps to good beekeeping are to learn about and understand the creatures you are dealing with and the natural world they inhabit. From then on, beekeeping is just like any other area of animal husbandry, all of which demand regular care and maintenance, time, skill and experience gained over the years. What makes bees different from many other creatures is that they remain wild insects. While we may make use of them, we must remember that they do not need us.

Getting honey from the hive to the honeypot will take a year of good management. On the first fine, warm day of the year the bees will emerge from the hive on a "cleansing flight" and begin to search for early nectar- and pollen-producing plants. Soon after, the beekeeper will inspect the hive for any winter damage and assess how strong the colony is. The queen should have started laying eggs in the brood cells and there should still be enough food left for the workers. Beekeepers use a smoker to calm the bees to make inspection easier. The smoke causes the bees to become drowsy and so less aggressive.

The Critical Time

A month or so later the egg cells should be well-stocked with eggs and larvae and plenty of "bee bread" or honey and pollen stocks. Extra honey may be provided as food and water if needed, and new frames inserted with fresh new wax foundation in place. Old debris and rubbish will be cleared away and re-queening done if necessary. The next few weeks may be critical if the weather suddenly turns cold, so the beekeeper watches and checks that the workers have been collecting enough food for all the newborn bees. By late spring the hive may swarm, which can mean a lot of work for the beekeeper. A swarm happens when most, or all, of a hive take off at once following the old queen. It is not completely clear why a colony swarms, but it may be because they are running out of room, or it is too hot inside the hive, or it may be nature's way of preventing disease by moving home. One main swarm will generally be followed by several more, depending on how many young queens there are left in the hive. The beekeeper will collect the swarm as soon as possible from its first stopping point, which is often on a branch of a tree, before the swarm can move on to a cavity or a more inaccessible final destination. Swarms give the beekeeper a good chance of starting a fresh hive or building up a weak colony.

Harvesting the Rewards

By early summer, the honey should be building up and all should be well with the bees. Hives may be moved through the season to catch a particular crop. Examples of this are hives moved into orchards for the tree blossom (a move which also helps the growers with fruit

A WBC hive (named after William Broughton Carr, who invented it early this century) stacked high with layers called supers, promising a large crop of honey later in the summer. The lowest super is the brood box and the four above it are for honey storage. Four of these is about the maximum to expect in one season.

❶ *This double walled WBC hive is very active with foraging bees. Twenty-four hours before taking honey a clearing board is put in place to stop bees going up into the super you wish to extract.*

❷ *The bees will know the honey is being taken and may get angry. It is essential to wear protective clothing, especially a hat and veil, which then gives the beekeeper the confidence to work easily and smoothly. First the lid is lifted off.*

This is a simple type of bee hat with black veil. Though mostly superseded by zip-on versions which can be attached to a boiler suit, this version is cheap and fairly effective as long as the ties are tight!

fertilization) or to moorlands for the heather flowers.

Oilseed rape honey has to be taken from the hive very soon after it has been collected, as it sets hard in the comb if left too long. Otherwise, the main honey harvest is usually later in the summer when the heavy frames are taken from the hive and the capping, or layer of wax sealing in the honey to each cell, is removed with a hot knife. Honey is generally taken from the frames by spinning the wax in a centrifugal extractor. It is then filtered and bottled. The wax may be cleaned and melted down for all kinds of other uses. A typical hive could yield up to 40kg (88lb) of honey, depending on the season and the strength of the colony. Traditionally, 24 August, or the feast of St Bartholomew, is the latest date for taking honey. From then on, the beekeeper checks his colonies, takes any action needed against disease and by early autumn starts to feed the bees with a sugar or honey solution. This gives them enough time to build stocks of honey for themselves through the winter months. The upper chambers are removed from the hive to concentrate the insects in a smaller space.

FROM THE HIVE TO THE HONEY POT

3 *Inside, the frames the bees have filled are exposed; you can see that a few stray bees are still present. Smoke is puffed into the hive which will keep the bees calm and less likely to attack. The bees on the frame can be brushed gently away; traditionally this is done with a goose feather.*

Smokers have not changed much in design over the years. Basically they consist of a chamber, which holds something combustible such as dry grass, corrugated card or old hessian sacking, and bellows to force the smoke through the funnel.

4 *Next the frames are lifted out and checked for honey. They are surprisingly heavy if full. Frames which are going to be harvested are taken indoors to a bee-tight room in case the insects follow. Before extracting honey the hive should be closed again and left in order.*

F R O M   T H E   H I V E   T O   T H E   H O N E Y   P O T

These frames with their new sheets of foundation wax are ready to go back into a super. There are ten frames per super in a WBC and eleven in a National hive. These frames are wired to give more support.

5 The top frame is completely filled with honey and each cell closed off with wax. This makes it easy to move around safely. The bottom frame has had all its wax and honey removed and a new wax foundation put in place.

6 The wax capping covering the comb is scraped off evenly to expose the liquid honey. A long-bladed knife is best for this. Then the frames are scraped or spun to remove the honey, which is usually filtered before bottling.

A galvanized metal honey extractor from the very early part of this century. Hand cranked machines have altered very little though now they tend to be made from plastic. A machine like this would take up to four frames at a time.

Examples of clear liquid honey. The darker one is a tree blossom honey and the paler one a mixed wild flower honey. Both are crystal clear and runny, but in time will naturally crystallize unless heat treated.

The Story of Honey

Honey and bees are mentioned as far back in time as we are able to go. The history of honey is a fascinating exploration covering every aspect of human life.

Representations of bees figured frequently in Egyptian hieroglyphs. These appear on an obelisk at the temple of Karnak.

Plutarch, the celebrated Greek biographer and philosopher, who travelled the length and breadth of Britain in the second century AD, remarked that "These Britons only begin to grow old at 120 years of age" and connected their long life to the amount of mead they drank.

The date when man enjoyed his first taste of honey is not known – we can only surmise that the earliest hunter–gatherers must have come cross a wild bees' nest in a hollow tree or bank of soil and plundered it. A few bee stings would be quickly forgotten, but the sweetness of the honey would remain in the memory, in contrast to their normally unpalatable diet of game, plants and nuts.

The Neolithic revolution, when man progressed from hunting to farming and stockbreeding, was a slow business and happened at different speeds in various parts of the world. As the glaciers receded, from around 12,000 BC, the climate gradually warmed up, resulting in the widespread colonisation of fast-growing plants, such as wild grains. Settlements were built near these plentiful wild crops and it slowly became clear that some seeds could be retained from one harvest and sown to produce another.

Around the same time, animals began to be herded and domesticated and, wherever the conditions were right, bees were taken from the wild and kept in primitive hives to provide honey and beeswax. The earliest illustration we have of honey being gathered is in a wall painting around 15,000 years old which appears on the walls of rock shelter in Eastern Spain.

It is thought that the nomadic people of central Asia may have introduced honey to the world, as many of its early names seem to have similar origins. The Sanskrit word *madhu*

In this prehistoric wall painting a female figure appears to have angered the bees in her attempt to extract

and the Chinese *myit* have echoes in the Slav word *medhu* and the English word *mead*.

The Egyptians and Greeks

Honey was a vital commodity for the ancient Egyptians, who used it as a food, as an offering to their gods and as an ingredient in embalming fluids. During the First Dynasty in Lower Egypt, around 320 BC, the bee became the symbol of the pharaoh and was used to represent his kingdom. From then on, the bee was regularly used to symbolise royalty in the hieroglyphs of the time. It is not hard to understand how people felt about the bee and its capacity to create something in such quantity from very little. In the days before biology and botany were understood, people must have

The Story of Honey

thought it was a special kind of magic which turned flower nectar into honey.

The Egyptians kept their bees in tall, cylindrical hives: similar hives of this type are still used in remote parts of Egypt today. The honey was collected by smoking one end of the cylinder to drive the bees to the opposite one, a method illustrated in tomb reliefs from this period. About half the honeycomb was then removed and the bees left alone again.

Beeswax was also of great importance – it was used for cosmetics and embalming as well as for writing tablets and encaustic painting: a method whereby pigments and resins were added to molten, bleached wax, which was then applied with a knife to a suitable surface. Heat was applied to set the colours and make the paint permanent. Encaustic painting was much used by the Egyptians, particularly for decorating the life-size portrait of the face on wood which was laid on the face of a mummy.

The Egyptians sometimes paid taxes in honey, and bee-keepers were taxed on their bounty. Great quantities of it were used as sacrifices, gifts to the gods and as grave goods to accompany kings to the afterlife. Records show that in the twelfth century BC, the king of Egypt, Rameses III, sacrificed 15 tons of honey to the Nile god Hapi – a staggering amount. Honey was also baked into special honey cakes, which were used as offering to placate the gods throughout ancient Egypt. A painted relief from the tomb of Rekh-mi-re, built around 1450 BC, shows a line of Egyptian bakers making the cakes and putting them in a clay oven. Some uneaten cakes from this period have been found, but how effective they were at pleasing the gods, we shall never know!

The Greeks also made little honey cakes from flour, honey and oil, sometimes baked with fresh flowers inside them, as supplications to their gods. They considered honey to be an

Honey was a vital commodity in Egyptian culture and commerce. This papyrus from 1258 BC shows Ani, a scribe, and his wife Tutu making an offering to the god Osiris which would certainly have contained honey.

The Story of Honey

Pliny the Elder wrote at length about bees in Historia Naturalis, *from which this illuminated initial, showing a beehive besieged by ants, is taken.*

The Romans loved honey and used it extensively in cooking. This pavement mosaic from the first century shows a typical banquet.

important food as well as a healing medicine; Greek recipe books of the time seemed to abound with all kinds of irresistible sweetmeats and cakes made from honey. Goat or sheep milk cheeses were mixed with it to make cheesecakes, described by Euripides in the fifth century BC as being "steeped most thoroughly in the rich honey of the golden bee".

There are numerous pieces of Greek literature on the subject, such as this early one from Hesiod, writing in 700 BC: "Every day the bees work eagerly all throughout the day till sundown and set the white combs, while the drones stay within the roofed hives and gather into their bellies the toils of others". Beekeeping was seen as a noble and worthwhile pastime, and the keeping of bees was widespread among rich and poor.

When in Rome

Later, in ancient Rome, hives were made from all kinds of substances. Pliny writes about the various merits of different materials, including bark, fennel plant and withies (willow twigs). He also describes a transparent material, believed to have been mica, used in hives so that the workings of the bees could be seen from the outside. Other materials included cork, logs, dung, brick, wood and earthenware. For his part, the first-century BC Roman poet Virgil recommended in the *Ecologues* that the hives should be weatherproofed against the winter and protected from the fierce summer sun by using mud smoothed over the outer surface.

Like the ancient Greeks, the Romans loved the taste of honey in their food and used it as a gift to their gods, so beekeeping flourished throughout the Roman empire. In the first century AD, Apicius, a wealthy gourmet (though some called him a glutton) wrote a series of books in which more than half the recipes included honey. He used it not just in sweet dishes, but with ingredients such as meat, fish, vegetables and nuts. Some of the recipes are exotic and inventive, to say the least: sweet melon with a savoury sauce made from crushed pepper, herbs and honey, followed by peacock marinaded in herbs and almonds and served with a honey, wine and vinegar sauce. Whole hams were salted and smoked, boiled with figs and bay leaves, the skin scored and rubbed with honey and the result finally baked whole in an

The Story of Honey

These charming bees appeared on a French sixteenth-century manuscript.

oven, much as we might cook a ham today. Plainer foods were more commonly eaten, particularly a kind of cake-like bread known as *panis mellitus* (honey bread).

Bees in the Woods

Central Europe had the perfect climate and environment for the production of honey. Thickly forested areas and a diversity of plant life meant good forage and cover for the bees. Poland and Germany, in particular, made great use of the products of the hive for food and drink. During a trip to the river Danube in the fifth century BC, Herodotus, a much-travelled Greek historian, wrote that he found the river almost uncrossable at one point because of the concentration of bees gathered there. Once Christianity had become established, honey and beeswax production increased still further, partly to keep up with the enormous demand for church candles. This was to decrease suddenly, however, at the start of the Reformation many centuries later.

Taxes were often demanded in honey or beeswax. Charlemagne, king of the Franks from AD 771 to AD 814, instructed farmers to keep bees expressly for the purpose of paying tax, demanding two-thirds of their honey and one-third of their wax. French bureaucracy continued to be hard on the honey producers at various times through history, putting a tax both on beehives and on the common practice of honey hunting during the medieval period. In 1791, the French revolutionary government demanded a precise record of every hive in the country, resulting in a wholesale reduction in commercial beekeeping. And as late as 1934 a tax was yet again put on hives, supposedly to assess beekeeping along with the farming.

Drinking Honey

Long before the Roman invasion of Britain, the island was described by early Druid bards as "The Isle of Honey". Once the Romans arrived on the scene, Pliny commented that "these islanders consume copious quantities of the honeybrew". In fact, most of the population of central Europe drank brews of various kinds based on honey. Mead was an everyday drink when water was unsafe and tea and coffee were still unheard of. Russia had its own version of mead, plus a variant called *kvas*, made from barley or rye, salt and a little honey. Mixed with

The dangers of disturbing the bees while extracting the honey can be seen in this thirteenth-century manuscript.

This nineteenth-century German print shows the process of straining honey into settling tanks to clear it. Although honey was less popular than sugar at this period, the tradition of beekeeping continued on a small scale.

The role of honey in medicine was achnowledged in A Compleat History of Drugs *by Pomet, published in London in 1725, as this plate from it shows.*

water and kept warm overnight, the mixture was stirred and left for a few more days until it was ready to drink. The result was refreshing and almost non-alcoholic, quite unlike mead.

Honey continued to be of vital importance to Europeans until the Renaissance, when the gradual influx of sugar from further afield meant less and less honey was used. By the seventeenth century, sugar was well-established as a sweetener and honey lost further ground. Once grain and hop-based ale became popular, the role of honey was minimal.

But in the New World, honey was gathering strength. The early settlers travelling to North America in the seventeenth century had taken hives of bees with them to provide valuable honey and beeswax. The insects adapted very well to the environment in Virginia and Massachusetts – the first areas to be colonized – and slowly spread west across the whole continent, reaching California by 1830. The country was already home to some indigenous types of bee, from which the native people took honey for cooking purposes.

Domestic bees were shipped to Australia, in the 1800s, after a long and arduous journey following Captain Cook's route in the *Isabella*. These bees thrived on the Australian climate and rapidly multiplied, becoming the basis of a thriving modern honey industry. Today, North America and Australia dominate the world's production and export of honey.

Bee Emblems

Over the centuries people of different cultures and religions have believed bees possess special attributes and powers, so have taken the bee as their emblem. From the First Dynasty (3,200 BC) the bee was the sign of the king of Lower Egypt, and drawings and engravings of a single stylized bee are frequently found in tombs and on statues, wall paintings and so on. The coffin of Men-Kau-ra (Fourth Dynasty, circa 2,500 BC) in the British Museum is one of the many early examples.

The Greeks called bees Birds of the Muse, because of their power to confer the gift of eloquence, and the Christian church believed bees to have strength and integrity because they swarmed away after the fall of man in the Garden of Eden. Mohammed viewed the bee with deference because, he claimed, the bee was the only animal who was addressed by the Lord himself.
Later historical figures who chose the bee as their emblem were Pope Urban VIII, and Napoleon.

The emblem of Urban VIII, the 239th Pope, on the Basilica of St Peter's in Rome.

Napoleon, resplendent in a robe decorated with his chosen emblem of single bees. His flag is cross-banded with a single line of bees in flight.

Health and Beauty

From the ancient Greek physicians to the followers of alternative medicine today, honey has always played an important role in the pursuit of health and beauty.

In the first century BC Hippocrates, the so-called father of modern medicine, praised honey's healing powers and regularly prescribed it to his patients. He formulated many honey-based cures for problems ranging from skin disorders, ulcers and sores to sweating, respiratory complaints and fevers.

Honey has always been enjoyed for its delicious taste, but it has also long been highly prized for its therapeutic and medicinal value. In the Old Testament Solomon advises "My son, eat thou honey" and the Koran proclaims that honey is "a medicine for men". Worldwide, it has been used in traditional forms of medicine and healing for as long as it has been taken from wild nests or domesticated hives. For less serious skin complaints, or simply to enhance beauty, honey has also been an important ingredient in cosmetics and beauty aids of all kinds.

Honey as a substance is quite complex. As a food, it contains 38 per cent fructose, 31 per cent glucose, 2 per cent sucrose (all natural sugars) and 17 per cent water. Natural honey will also contain small amounts of vitamins, such as thiamin, ascorbic acid, riboflavin, pantygiothenic acid, rydoxine and niacin, but over-zealous filtering and heating can destroy these. Depending on the plants visited by the bees, the honey produced may also contain varying amounts of other substances, such as the mineral potassium, amino acids and plant acids. It is thought that some specific flower honeys may have special properties because of substances in the nectar: eucalyptus honey, for example, may help in chest and respiratory complaints in the same way as eucalyptus oil from the tree.

One long-standing use of honey (recorded from as early as 2500 BC and still used today) is in the treatment of wounds and burns to the skin. The ancient Egyptians used honey in very many different medicines, but one particular document gives instructions for placing honey directly onto the affected part of the body and wrapping it round with cloth as a dressing. This was used for open wounds, cuts, burns or ulcers and if successful, the wound would dry out and heal satisfactorily with the minimum of scarring. The honey certainly forms a barrier to further infection from outside and in fact sugar has been used for a similar purpose.

On the Battlefield

It is believed that honey has the property of drawing out water from the cells of bacteria, causing them to dehydrate and die. It also contains an antibiotic substance called inhibine. As recently as the First World War German doctors were using honey mixed with cod liver oil to surgically dress wounds on the battlefront, and in some Eastern European countries the medical professions are still using it today.

It is difficult to substantiate much of the fact surrounding honey's healing properties and there is still great scepticism about many of the fantastic claims made by honey's advocates. There is no doubt, however, that honey has stood the test of time. Much has been written

---

Sleep Enticer

The combination of chamomile, a natural sedative, and honey, believed to induce sleep, should result in a peaceful, uninterrupted slumber. The beverage is best sipped when tucked up in bed, propped up with a good book so that you can drift off to sleep.

1 chamomile tea infusion bag
2tsp honey

Make a cup of chamomile tea with hot water and allow to cool until warm only. Stir in the honey and sip intermittently.

HEALTH AND BEAUTY

A near contemporary of Hippocrates, Democritus (the philosopher and physician) tried out many diets himself in the search for a formula for eternal life. He chose a diet with honey as an important part of it and supposedly lived until he was 109 years old.

Herbal Cold and Throat Syrup

To relieve all those irritating symptoms that accompany a cold, try this syrup. Sage is said to alleviate aches, pains and fever.

½tsp chopped fresh or
rubbed dried sage
3tbsp honey
2tbsp cider vinegar

Tie the sage in a muslin bag and steep in a cup half filled with boiling water for 10 minutes. Remove the sage and allow to cool.
Put the honey in a screwtop jar or bottle. Pour in the cider vinegar then pour in the cooled sage water. Shake until well mixed.
Take 2 teaspoons every hour until the symptoms ease.

Propolis, or "beeglue", a by-product of honey, is gleaned from sticky plants and used in the hive to fill cracks and holes. Its anti-fungal and anti-septic properties make it a useful remedy for minor skin complaints.

Health and Beauty

Dioscorides worked as a physician in Greece in the first century AD. He claimed great powers for honey as a medicine prescribing it for coughs, as a diuretic, for treating young and old alike and even for cases of poisoning by mushroom, snake bite or rabid dog.

Velvety Honey Conditioner

Based on an early eighteenth century recipe secretly devised by Queen Anne, this enriching, creamy treatment will condition your hair and give it shine as well as leaving it velvety soft. Adding a couple of teaspoons of lemon juice will have a brightening effect on blond hair. The conditioner needs to be mixed just before it is needed, as otherwise it will separate before you are ready to use it.

2tbsp creamy set honey
1tbsp olive oil
1/4tsp vanilla essence

Wash your hair as usual and towel it dry until just damp.
Place all the ingredients in a bowl and mix together using a whisk; alternatively place the ingredients in a screwtop jar and shake vigorously. Smooth the conditioner liberally over the hair, combing it through with a wide-toothed comb to make sure it is evenly applied. Cover your head with a thin plastic shower cap. Warm your hair using a hairdrier for about five minutes; the heat causes the conditioner to penetrate the hair. Relax for 15 minutes then remove the plastic cap and wash off the conditioner with a small amount of mild shampoo to remove excess oils.

over the centuries about its ability to heal wounds. A book of cures from the eighteenth century describes an episode where a woman in Rome suffered terrible burns over most of her body after her clothes caught alight. A servant hastily covered her burns with honey and nine days later, according to the text, she was "perfectly cured by this remedy alone". An American doctor researching into the healing of wounds with honey wrote in 1973 that he had found "that honey when applied every two or three days under a dressing promotes the healing of wounds and ulcers better than any other local application I have ever used."

We are unlikely to find out how much truth, if any, there is in such claims until proper studies and research are carried out. As is the case with much "alternative" medicine, little research will be done while there are mass-produced, effective drugs available. However, as we move towards a time where many bacteria and diseases show signs of becoming immune to modern drugs, some practitioners believe natural healers will be taken more seriously.

Health and Beauty

One use for honey which most of us will probably have enjoyed and benefited from is as a soothing medicine for sore throats or irritating coughs. Honey had long been used as a sweet disguise for unpleasant-tasting medicines: being liquid, it mixed well with other ingredients and hid any bitterness or bad taste. There are delicious-sounding recipes for honey mixed with chopped sweet-scented rose or violet petals from medieval times. The rose version, known as "melrosette", was given as a medicine; although roses were essentially sweet and comforting, they were also seen as a cure for many kinds of ills. Most medieval honey mixtures had vile-tasting purging herbs, such as wormwood or rue, added to them so roses and violets were probably the attractive exception.

Coughs and colds

Dorothy Hartley, in her book *Food in England* describes how country children who had ticklish coughs and sore throats were soothed by being given little balls of granulated honey creamed with butter. They would let the sweet rich mixture slowly dissolve in their mouths. Alison Uttley, the childrens' author, grew up in Derbyshire on a farm at the end of the last century and remembers morsels of butter, honey and lemon being prescribed for a cold. She describes a cough medicine made from salad oil, paregoric (a camphor mixture), lemon juice and honey. Today, all manner of commercial cough soothers are still based around honey and are generally combined with lemon juice to provide a dose of vitamin C. The traditional hot lemon, honey and whisky cold

Hangover Cure

After over-indulgence in alcohol, the second half of this recipe is useful for reducing unwanted hangover symptoms. However, if you know in advance that there is a possibility you might drink too much, take the first part of the cure before leaving home for the best results.

2½tbsp honey
150ml/5fl oz milk
1 lemon, juice only

Mix 1 tablespoon of the honey with the milk, and drink this before any anticipated over-indulgence of alcohol to line the stomach.
On returning home, mix the remainder of the honey with the lemon juice and 150ml/5fl oz water to accelerate the liver's processing rate.

Lemon and Honey Throat Soother

An old favourite, this concoction is effective for treating mild sore throats. It can be used as a gargle to soothe the throat, and can then be swallowed to gain maximum benefit from the ingredients. If you omit the ginger the mixture makes a good cough mixture, to be taken one teaspoon at a time as needed.

3tbsp honey
1 lemon, juice only
2tsp vegetable glycerine
¼tsp ground ginger

Place the honey and lemon in a small bowl and stir until well mixed. Add the vegetable glycerine, stirring until smooth. Stir in the ginger. Gargle and swallow 1 teaspoon every hour.

A tincture of propolis is used as a natural infection fighter against such problems as sore throats, the common cold, and mouth and gum disorders. At one time violin makers used propolis in their wood varnish.

Poppea, the beloved wife of the Emperor Nero, instructed her servants to regularly put a mixture of honey and asses' milk on her face to keep the skin smooth and youthful.

Propolis has been claimed to have all kinds of beneficial properties. Here it has found its way into a natural toothpaste.

cure is as popular as ever, with good reason, but try the Herbal Cold and Throat Remedy or the Lemon and Honey Throat Soother if you prefer a different non-alcoholic version. If all the ingredients are not at hand when you develop a sudden cough or sore throat, try taking a spoonful of liquid honey and swallow it slowly, letting it get to work on the painful throat.

These all seem to be rather delicious medicines, but an old traditional English remedy for earache is certainly one to avoid. A small piece of peeled onion was dipped in honey and inserted into the ear – how long it was left there is uncertain! There may have been some common sense in this, though, as onion is a known antiseptic. However, the risk of further infection outweighs the potential benefits from this rather unappealing cure.

There have long been claims that honey can be beneficial to sufferers of chest complaints such as asthma and bronchitis. Tests carried out at the Medical Research Department at Lansing in Michigan, USA after the Second World War found that hay fever sufferers appeared to benefit from a diet which included honey, especially if small amounts of pollen were still in the unrefined honey. The researchers also noticed that chewing the honey-filled comb had an even more beneficial effect. Some alternative health practitioners suggest a course of pollen-rich local honey before the hay fever season begins, as a way of boosting resistance to the affecting pollen.

Beeswax, too, has long been used as a primitive kind of chewing gum. There are medieval recipes for it combining wax, honey, ginger and cinnamon with oil of terebinth, which came from fir trees and gave the gum a resinous pine flavour.

And so to bed

Honey reputedly also has a soporific effect, so has often been used to make sleep-inducing potions. Gipsy recipes, for example, use the juice of lemons and oranges mixed with honey and diluted with hot water, to be drunk before retiring for the night. That well known sleep promoter, warm milk, is supposed to have an even faster effect if sweetened with a spoonful of honey but it is not really surprising that such a concoction might induce sleep. Milk and honey is the stuff of myth and legend, and on a more basic level a mug of it is likely to remind us of carefree childhood bedtimes or even

A fine skin was considered essential by the Egyptians. This relief from Denderah shows Cleopatra exposing more than a little of hers but it would have been softened and smoothed by baths of honey and asses' milk.

Cleansing Morning Tonic

There is no better way to start the day than with this refreshing tonic. The benefits are several: it cleans out the system; it is a mild laxative; it promotes a healthy, well-functioning liver; and it is good for skin blemishes. For maximum benefit, take this tonic every morning before breakfast.

3tsp honey
1/2 lemon, juice only

Mix the honey and lemon juice with 150ml/5fl oz of lukewarm water, and drink.

Health and Beauty

Rich Honey Hand Balm

Ideal for soothing dry hands, this moisturizing, satiny, rose-scented balm uses beeswax to protect skin from adverse conditions, and olive oil to give extra smoothness. It is also good for restoring moisture to tired hands, rough elbows or chapped lips. Beeswax granules are available from health food shops.

1tsp beeswax granules
½tsp olive oil
1tbsp honey
1–2 drops rose essential oil

Place the beeswax granules and olive oil in a small bowl set over a saucepan of simmering water. Allow the wax to melt then turn off the heat. With the bowl still set over the saucepan, quickly stir in the honey and rose oil. Stir until smooth then pour into a small jar and allow to set. When it is just warm, stir with your finger or the handle of a spoon until creamy.
To use, first place your hands or elbows in warm water and dry them; the balm is easier to apply on to warmed skin. Place a dab of balm in your palm and massage in to the skin until your hands feel smooth and soft. Remove excess balm with a tissue.
For your lips, simply apply with your fingertips or a lip brush.

sleepy babyhood hours at the breast or bottle. The physicians of ancient Rome used honey to help their patients get to sleep and were so impressed by its potency that they felt obliged to warn patients of its potential strength, lest they did not wake up at daybreak. Of course, this might just have been a clever way of absolving themselves from any blame should their patients die in their sleep due to the physician's negligence.

The Romans believed that honey had a tonic effect on the whole gastrointestinal area and prescribed it as a gentle but efficient laxative – and oddly, as a cure for diarrhoea too. Research has been carried out on the use of honey as a treatment for diarrhoea, with claims that common gut bacteria such as salmonella, chigella and *E. coli* cannot survive in honey. (This may be the same principle as preserving foods with sugar so that the bacteria cannot survive in the concentrated sweet environment.)

The energy giver

By the seventeenth century in Britain, ideas about the beneficial medicinal uses of honey were quite wide-ranging. Often based on writings of the Greeks and other ancients, few facts could be scientifically proven, but would come from observation, experience and the research of others. In 1623, a keen British beekeeper called Charles Butler wrote a book called *History of Bees*. Based on the writings of a first century Greek physician known as Dioscorides, Butler claimed that "Honey clears up all the instructions of the body, loosens the belly, purges the foulness of the body, provokes urine, cuts down phlegm, restores the appetite, takes away that which damages the eyes and nourishes very much". He went on to say that it bred good blood, preserved natural heat and prolonged life.

Marguerite de Navarre, wife of King Henri IV of France, was one of many French beauties who swore by the regular use of honey to maintain her beautiful complexion.

Health and Beauty

Agnes Sorel, the mistress of Charles VII of France, was known as la Dame de Beauté from the name of the estate the besotted King gave her. She was a passionate advocate of honey both as a cosmetic and in the form of a spice cake invented in honour of Charles at Dijon containing strong buckwheat honey from Brittany.

Commercial versions of honey water for the hair were obviously available early this century. This one is described as a wash and a pomade. A pomade was more likely to be used by a man as a dressing or treatment for the hair rather like brilliantine.

Interestingly, all these claims for honey seem to have been popular at one time or another in various countries and cultures. That honey is nourishing is well known and athletes, from runners in the original Olympic Games in ancient Greece to modern-day climbers and English Channel swimmers have taken advantage of its speedy energy-boosting qualities. Because honey is made up of fructose and glucose, it has a two-tier energy supply. The glucose is quickly absorbed by the body and gives an immediate boost, while the fructose works more slowly to provide a sustained amount of energy. Experiments on athletes earlier this century in Toronto showed that those who took honey before and after competing recovered more quickly from their exertions than those who relied on other forms of sugar. Being an alkaline food, honey is broken down by saliva more quickly during the first stage of digestion within the mouth. Additionally, both glucose and fructose are

Geranium Softening Facial

The geranium oil in this penetrating facial mask improves the blood circulation around the face, giving it a healthy glow. The mask softens and hydrates the skin, leaving it smooth and silky.

*2tbsp whipping cream
1 size 2 egg, yolk only
1tbsp creamy set honey
1–2 drops geranium essential oil*

In a bowl, whisk the cream until it is beginning to thicken and soft peaks are just forming. Whisk in the egg yolk until fluffy then add the honey and geranium essential oil, whisking until evenly blended.
Using a large cosmetic or blusher brush, apply the mixture to your face and neck. Relax for 20 minutes while the mask does its work. Rinse the mask off with warm water and splash your face and neck with cold water or toner to tighten the pores.

Health and Beauty

Fragrant Lemon Deep-Cleansing Treatment

Fresh and deep-cleansing, this treatment opens skin pores and refines the complexion. It is ideal as a preparation before applying a deep-cleansing mask treatment.

1tbsp clear honey
2–3 drops lemon essential oil

Using a large cosmetic brush or wet fingertips, apply the honey thinly to your face and relax for 10 minutes to allow the honey time to soften the skin. When ready, pour boiling water into a bowl and add the lemon essential oil. Lean over the bowl and place a towel over your head and the bowl so that the steam can work on your pores. When the steam stops rising, rinse off any honey left on the skin. Finally, splash your face with cold water to close the pores.

said to be highly digestible. It appears that bees have already done some of the work for our alimentary system by partially digesting the sugars themselves, so the honey is quickly and easily absorbed by our bodies without any irritation to our digestive system. That honey "prolongs life" is another claim that has been widely held over the centuries with a few cases of people reaching an amazing age and citing honey as the cause of their longevity. The ancient Greek physician Hippocrates was convinced of honey's ability to prolong life and his near contemporary, the philosopher and physicist Democritus, supposedly managed to live for 109 years thanks to following a diet based on honey.

Bathing in beauty

Honey may or may not be a dietary formula for eternal youth, but when added to cosmetics, it has long been used to delay or counteract the effects of ageing on the skin. It would appear that its healing properties, harnessed so dramatically for the treatment of wounds, can also help in day-to-day skin care for face, hands and body. There are many references over the centuries to the use of honey as a cosmetic, particularly by the rich and powerful women of their time. Whether it was also more commonly used by the mass of people it is harder to discover, though presumably ordinary people with access to honey might have accidentally discovered how soft and smooth their hands became after contact with it.

Cleopatra is remembered for her famous baths of asses' milk, which supposedly contained honey. Bath is probably the wrong word for this beauty treatment, since a further washing must have been needed to remove the sweet stickiness from her skin. Poppea, the wife of the Roman emperor Nero, also used the honey skin treatment, and regularly instructed her servants to smear a honey and milk lotion over her face to keep her looking youthful. Chinese women have a tradition of using a blend of honey and ground orange pips to keep their skins blemish-free, and in Japan honey was used as a softening hand lotion. The French have always been dedicated to the pursuit of beauty and many famous French women from every century seem to have used honey as part of their toilette. Agnes Sorrel, the

It is claimed that Queen Anne used a honey and oil concoction to keep her long hair lustrous, thick and shiny. In this portrait she has her hair long and natural in the romantic style of the early 1700s.

HEALTH AND BEAUTY

Madame du Barry is served her morning chocolate looking elegant and perfectly coiffed. Writings of the period tell us that her skin benefited from frequent applications of honey.

Oatmeal Exfoliating Mask

The combination of honey and oatmeal makes the perfect treatment for a dull or oily skin. The mask is gently removed after the treatment, lifting off dead skin cells and leaving the complexion clear and fresh.

1 size 2 egg, yolk only
2tbsp clear honey
3tbsp finely ground oatmeal
1tsp orange water

In a bowl, whisk together the egg yolk and honey until velvety. Sprinkle in the oatmeal and blend well. Finally, add the orange water to scent the mixture.
Using a large cosmetic brush, paint the oatmeal over your face and neck to completely cover them, avoiding the eyes. Relax with a good book or lie down for 20 minutes.
When the treatment has taken effect, gently rub your face and neck with your fingertips to loosen the oatmeal mask.
Remove the mask with a facecloth or cotton pads moistened with warm water.

mistress of Charles VII, used it in the fifteenth century and called it "the soul of flowers". Coincidentally, she also had a passion for honey in a different form – in spiced bread, of which she claimed she would never tire. Madame du Barry, the infamous last mistress of Louis XV, used honey as a form of facial mask, lying down for a rest while the honey did its work. Later, the honey was rinsed away with warm water – an idea we could copy, but one which is probably best done while in the bath. Try the Geranium Softening Facial (page 32) when your face needs pampering.

Honey and Buttermilk Cleanser

Made from honey and buttermilk with a dash of rosewater, this cleanser is inspired by the famous beauty treatment used by Cleopatra and many other beautiful women in history. It will leave the skin feeling refreshed, silky soft and clean.

2tsp clear honey
1tbsp buttermilk
¼tsp rosewater

Whisk all the ingredients together in a bowl and apply the cleanser to your face, neck and shoulders using your fingertips. Splash off with lukewarm water, then pat the skin dry.

Most research into the uses of honey as a beauty preparation suggest that it was used mainly for skin treatments, but there are records of it being made into hair lotions and tonics too. In England Queen Anne, who was said to have taken enormous pride in her appearance, invented a preparation to keep her hair healthy and lustrous. As none of her ladies-in-waiting dared to risk asking her for the secret, it was not revealed until her death in 1714. Her hair conditioner consisted of honey beaten with olive oil of, no doubt, the finest quality. It reputedly gave her hair a marvellous shine and has been used by women in some form or other ever

HEALTH AND BEAUTY

Lavender Tightening Facial Mask

Wonderfully fragrant, this mask will tighten skin, leaving it silky but taut. It is a good, quick facial pick-me-up before an important night out.

1tbsp clear honey
2tsp thick yoghurt
1 size 2 egg, white only
2–3 drops lavender essence

In a bowl, whisk the honey and yoghurt together until smooth and well blended. Add the egg white and lavender essence, mixing until silky smooth.
Using a cosmetic brush or your fingertips, smooth the mask over your face, taking care to avoid the eye and lip areas. Leave the mask in place for 10–15 minutes; you will feel the tightening effect on your skin as it dries.
Rinse the mask off with lukewarm water, and splash your face with your favourite toner or flower water.

Honey water has been popular as a face freshener or tonic for centuries.

since. Try the recipe for Velvety Honey Conditioner (page 28) for yourself. Another English beauty, Sarah, Duchess of Marlborough, was also credited with having beautiful hair. Judging by portrait paintings of the time, a woman's hair was expected to be long, natural looking and romantically swept into gentle curls. (This was before the era of outrageous powdered artificial wigs.) A contemporary of the Duchess once wrote of her that "she had the most beautiful head of hair imaginable, the colour of which she had preserved unchanged by the constant use of honey water". Sarah and Anne had been firm friends until they fell out in later life. So perhaps they shared the secret of using honey to keep their hair in beautiful condition.

By the time cosmetics were beginning to be mass-produced at the end of the nineteenth century, honey was a popular ingredient. Then, as now, its connotations of naturalness, the outdoors and good health made it attractive. Beeswax has also always been used as an emulsifying agent and an important ingredient of creams and lotions as it is a pure and easily obtainable, though expensive, product. It is included in the recipe for rich Honey Hand Balm. The simplest uses of honey are often the best. For example, a mixture of ground almonds, oatmeal, honey and egg yolk makes a marvellous cleanser and softener for hard worked hands that have been gardening or doing too much housework. Or try a similar recipe for Oatmeal Exfoliating Mask, this time for the face.

An engraving of one of many portraits made of Sarah, Duchess of Marlborough who was famed for the beauty of her hair. It was claimed that she used her own secret recipe for a honey water to keep it in such good condition.

A World of Honey

Many shops and supermarkets now stock a wide range of honeys and the displays in specialist shops can be bewildering, especially for the novice. Honeys range in colour from almost white to nearly black; they may be clear or opaque and, while some of their names are comfortingly recognisable, some are exotic and strange. Fortunately, things are not as complicated as they might appear at first glance.

Clear honey is fairly fluid and is in virtually the same state as it was in the hive. It has only been strained through a cloth or fine mesh to remove any debris. Occasionally it is heat-treated to prevent crystallization. It is usually a lovely pale or golden amber colour, but can be darker, even almost black, depending on the flowers from which it was made.

Creamy set honey is thick and opaque. It is granulated honey from which some of the moisture has been removed. The colour of this type of honey ranges from almost white to creamy, to dark yellow. Creamy set honeys are easy to spread – just right for hot toast.

All honeys are sweet, but when it comes to tasting them individually it is surprising how much range there is. The range of scents and flavours is also astonishing, and depends on the type of flowers used by the bees. Some flavours are distinctive, others only just subtly different from the next.

A honey is termed multi-flower if the bees were allowed to pick and choose the nectar from a range of vegetation, making up their own unique recipe. Single-flower honey may sound simpler, but it requires more skill on the part of the beekeeper to ensure that the bees take the nectar largely from one specific type of flower; there will always be a stray blossom or two along the route the bee travels. One way to do this is to physically transport the hives to the place where a particular flower or crop is in blossom, and leave them there until the flowering is over. The honey has to be harvested before the hive is moved on to another spot, perhaps as a different crop comes into flower. The other way to ensure single-flower honey is for the beekeeper to be so totally in tune with the seasons as to know just when a particular type of plant is in flower and, therefore, possibly dominant. As soon as the flowering of that particular plant is over, to the day, the beekeeper must remove the honey.

Blended honey is made up of several varieties. Blending honeys is a little like blending wines, and is a way of creating a uniform honey from undistinguished harvests, with a sustainable texture and flavour that will appeal to a wide audience. To do this requires some skill in identifying bouquet, assessing colour and savouring flavour. A professional honey taster or blender can "nose" a honey to identify the flower and assess the flavour.

Cut comb honey is just what it says: a piece of the comb with honey still in the cells cut and packed into a jar with pale liquid honey poured round it. You get the wax, honey, pollen – and any other bits and pieces!

Selection honey is sold as a complete square or block of comb contained in a small wooden frame packaged into a box or wrapped securely in cellophane. This is difficult to produce commercially and is nowadays quite a rarity. Consequently, it has become a luxury.

The honeybee has a fantastic array of flowers at its disposal. In theory, anything that contains nectar is worth investigating, but which blossoms a bee or group of bees decides to home in on will depend upon local availability at a given time of year and preference.

These bees have been irresistably attracted to this jar of honey, even though the honey itself has been processed, and is no longer in the pure state they are used to in the hive.

As this sample shows, honeys can be either clear or creamy set, though a few partly granulated or crystallized varieties achieve a middle path between the two. Lighter-coloured honeys tend to be milder in flavour.

Acacia Honey
A clear honey produced in East Europe and many other parts of the world. It is a pale, light colour with a hint of gold and has a thin and runny consistency. Its flavour, of heavily scented flowers, is sweeter than that of most honeys.

Chestnut Honey
A clear honey from the French Pyrenees and northern Italy. The colour is a lovely dark reddish-gold and it has quite a thick consistency. The rich, nutty flavour of burnt roasted chestnuts has a slightly bitter, tannin-like undertone.

Buckwheat Honey
A clear honey made from the buckwheat crops of the USA and China. Extremely dark, almost black in colour, it has a thick consistency. The intense flavour is somewhat like treacle and it has a pungent, earthy aroma. It is often used in blends.

Greek Mountain Honey
A clear honey gathered in Greek mountains. It is a dark toffee-brown with a medium to thick consistency. Its wonderfully strong taste is of pine and herbs with a slightly medicinal undertone and its scent captures the rich bouquet of Mediterranean flowers and herbs.

Leatherwood Honey
A clear set honey unique to the west coast of Tasmania in Australia. Golden amber in colour, it has a medium to thin consistency. The flavour is reminiscent of the heady scent of flowers on a hot summer's day, and it has a highly perfumed aroma.

Heather Honey
Not quite clear and sometimes rather dense, this honey is gathered from the moorlands and open woodlands of northern and western Europe. Golden amber with red overtones, its slightly gelatinous texture makes it almost chewy. The flavour is mildly sweet, a little bitter and grassy, with a pleasing aftertaste of burnt caramel.

Clover Honey
A usually clear, but sometimes creamy, set honey, produced from ground flora grown as animal fodder in the UK, Canada, USA, Australia and New Zealand. It is light amber and has a fairly thin consistency. It is very sweet with a delicate, fresh mown lawn scent.

Lime Blossom Honey
A clear honey, usually from East Europe or the USA. It is a light amber colour with a greenish tinge and has a thin, runny consistency. Made from the blossom of the lime or linden tree, it has no connection with the citrus fruit lime. It has a strong, heady aroma and tang.

Eucalyptus Honey
A clear honey produced in Australia. It is quite dark in colour with a medium to thin consistency. Its distinctive taste, not as strong as the colour would suggest, is of dried sultanas mixed with the fresh, stringent scents of the Australian bush.

Lavender Honey
A clear honey, usually from areas bordering the Mediterranean, notably the Provence region of France. It is a pale golden colour with a medium consistency. The delicate flavour is reminiscent of lavender flowers and quite sweet, though it ends with a touch of tartness.

A World of Honey

Manuka Honey
A clear honey from the New Zealand manuka tree. It is a dense caramel brown with a fairly thick and sticky consistency, similar to that of heather honey. The unique flavour is medicinal, slightly bitter and tannin-like with caramel overtones.

Strawberry Clover Honey
A creamy set honey taken from the strawberry clover flower in South Australia. The colour is an unusual muddy, creamy white. Being very thick it is a little difficult to handle, but the sweet, buttery taste, reminiscent of caramels, makes any effort worthwhile.

Oilseed Rape Honey
A creamy set honey from the oilseed rape crop found throughout Europe. The colour is a yellow-tinged white and the consistency is very thin and runny. Very sweet and creamy tasting with a slightly oily aftertaste, it is often used in blends.

Thyme Honey
A clear honey from wild plants in the Provence region of France and the Greek mountains. It is a rich dark amber in colour with a medium consistency. The strong herb flavour has a slightly bitter aftertaste.

Canadian Clover Honey
A creamy set honey from Canada. It is rich, luscious creamy white with a velvety texture. Its medium consistency is just right for spreading. The flavour is reminiscent of vanilla, combined with the scent of beeswax candles.

Sunflower Honey
A creamy set honey from Europe. It has a rich creamy yellow colour and a very thick consistency, second only to that of strawberry clover. The flavour is mildly sweet, distinctly oily and waxy and reminiscent of the countryside.

Orange Blossom Honey
A superbly fragrant clear honey from Israel, Malta, Spain, the USA and Mexico. Light amber in colour and thin to medium in consistency, it is fairly sweet with a flavour full of almonds and orange rind.

Rosemary Honey
A clear herb honey from the Mediterranean. It has a lovely dense but light golden colour and a thick, slightly gelatinous consistency, similar to that of heather honey, with a tendency to crystallize. The taste is sweet and floral with a hint of the herb.

Tupelo Honey
A clear honey unique to Florida, USA. It is pale gold in colour and has a very thin and runny consistency. The delicate but fragrant taste is of spring flowers and is fairly sweet.

CHAPTER ONE

First Courses

Honey is a perfect ingredient in quick snacks and first courses, providing both an instant boost of energy and unusual flavours. From French toast dusted with cinnamon to prosciutto and aubergine crostini, honey can be the ingredient that transforms the conventional into the sublime.

First Courses

With the pace of modern life, a relaxed, formal meal is becoming more and more of a luxury. The starter sets the tone for the whole meal, so why restrict it to assorted salad leaves and croutons or limp prawn cocktails? Just add a touch of delicately flavoured honey to transform a simple vinaigrette. Or add orange juice and honey to create a bittersweet infusion to complement a classic chicory and orange salad.

For a teatime treat, indulge yourself with hot toasted muffins, crumpets or bagels spread with honey. Turn a simple yoghurt into a delicious and nutritious snack with a spoonful of honey and some chopped nuts, or fresh fruit – strawberries are ideal – chopped roughly and bathed in clear honey. For something a little more sophisticated, light pancakes smothered in honey and lemon are simply delicious.

Holyday, *James Tissot*, 1876

Smoked Trout *with* Mustard *and* Tarragon Sauce

Delicately flavoured acacia honey adds a certain sweetness and softness to the dressing in this dish. To achieve the best results, make the dressing an hour or so in advance and place it in a refrigerator to allow time for the tarragon to diffuse its flavour.

SERVES 4

2tbsp Dijon mustard
1tbsp acacia honey
3tsp tarragon-flavoured white wine vinegar
1tsp finely chopped fresh tarragon
4tbsp single cream
4 smoked trout fillets
150g • 5oz oak leaf lettuce, or similar leaves
salad or garden cress, snipped
freshly ground black pepper

To make the sauce, combine the mustard, honey and white wine vinegar in a small bowl. Mix until smooth then add the tarragon and stir in the cream.

Arrange the lettuce leaves on individual plates. Break up each trout fillet and distribute the flesh evenly over the lettuce leaves. Drizzle the mustard and tarragon dressing over then sprinkle with the snipped cress.

Season with freshly ground black pepper and serve.

Bears like Honey

In literature, bears and a love of honey are almost synonymous, one of the most famous fictional honey fans being A.A. Milne's Winnie the Pooh. In real life, bears like the Himalayan black bear and the Indian sloth bear will go to great lengths to indulge their taste, showing enormous ingenuity to reach even the remotest hives.

FIRST COURSES

Compote *of* Orange, Fig *and* Date *with a* Crunchy Granola

The sultana-like flavour of eucalyptus honey marries well with the fresh and dried fruits of this compote. Excellent as a breakfast dish, it can double as a dessert if you replace the pine nut granola with a portion of crème fraîche or Greek-style yoghurt. Dried figs can be used in place of fresh ones but will require longer cooking; add them to the syrup with the orange segments and dates.

SERVES 4

150g • 5oz eucalyptus honey
4tbsp orange-flavoured liqueur
5cm • 2in cinnamon stick
4 cloves
2 oranges, peeled, segmented and with pith removed
16 dried dates
4 fresh figs, halved
GRANOLA
30g • 1oz porridge oats
1tbsp pine nuts
1tbsp sunflower seeds

Place the honey, orange-flavoured liqueur, cinnamon stick and cloves in a saucepan with 120ml/4fl oz of water. Bring to the boil then simmer for 5-8 minutes until the liquid starts to thicken and become syrupy.

Add the orange segments and dates and simmer for 15 minutes. Add the figs and simmer for a further 5 minutes. Allow the compote to cool then chill in the refrigerator for at least 2 hours before serving.

To make the granola, heat a frying pan until hot then add the oats, pine nuts and sunflower seeds. Turn the heat down to medium and toast for about 1 minute until golden brown. Serve sprinkled over the compote.

Chilled Mint *and* Honey Soup *with* Poppadoms

Sweet and savoury flavours are successfully mixed in this chilled minty soup to make a refreshing summer dish and an interesting prelude to an Indian meal.

SERVES 4

60g • 2oz salted butter
4 shallots, roughly chopped
1 honeydew or any white-fleshed melon, seeded and chopped
400ml • 14fl oz vegetable stock
1tbsp clear honey
1¼tbsp white wine vinegar
10g • ⅓oz whole mint leaves
pinch salt
120ml • 4fl oz single cream
4tbsp Greek-style yoghurt
4 plain poppadoms, ready for cooking
1tbsp roughly chopped mint leaves for garnish

Melt the butter in a saucepan, add the shallots and sauté for 2-3 minutes until soft. Add the melon and cook for 2-3 minutes. Pour in the vegetable stock and simmer for about 5 minutes. Allow to cool.

Pour the contents of the saucepan into a food processor, add the honey, white wine vinegar and the whole mint leaves and blend until smooth. Add salt to taste.

Pour the mixture into a bowl, add the cream and 2 tablespoons of the yoghurt then whisk briefly. Chill in the freezer for 40-60 minutes before serving.

While the soup is chilling, cook the poppadoms. Place one at a time in a microwave oven on high for 30 seconds, or until it puffs up. Alternatively cook under a medium-hot grill for 1-2 minutes, turning halfway through cooking.

Remove the soup from the freezer and whisk lightly if settled. Serve in individual bowls topped with ½ tablespoon yoghurt and a sprinkling of chopped mint.

Dreaming of Honey

"Hide me from day's garish eye,
While the bee, with honeyed thigh,
That at her flowering work doth sing,
And the waters murmering,
with such consort as they keep,
Entice the dewy-feather'd sleep."

IL PENSEROSO, JOHN MILTON 1608-74

First Courses

Leek Terrine *with* Honey *and* Mustard Vinaigrette

Pink peppercorns delicately flavour this light, creamy terrine while honey adds sweetness to the vinaigrette, countering the acidity and making a smooth sauce. Served warm it will keep out the cold on cool days; chilled, it is perfect for a hot summer's day.

SERVES 4

- 1kg • 2lb leeks
- 60g • 2oz butter
- 3tbsp roughly chopped chives plus whole chives for garnish
- 3tbsp white wine
- 1tsp pink peppercorns
- 6tbsp single cream
- 1tsp Dijon mustard
- 2 size 2 eggs
- hot pepper sauce to taste

Vinaigrette
- 1tbsp Dijon mustard
- 1tbsp clear honey
- 1tsp pink peppercorns
- 2tbsp white wine vinegar
- 6tbsp olive oil
- freshly ground black pepper

Preheat the oven to 175°C/350°F/gas mark 4.
 Trim 4 of the leeks to fit lengthways in a 1 litre/1¾ pint loaf tin. Bring a saucepan of water to the boil and cook the trimmed leeks for 2-3 minutes until they start turning bright green and are slightly softened. Remove them from the pan and plunge them in cold water to stop the cooking process. Pat them dry with kitchen paper and set aside.
 Slice the remaining leeks into rounds. Melt the butter in a frying pan, add the sliced leeks and cook for 4-5 minutes until tender and soft. Allow to cool slightly then place in a food processor with the chopped chives, the white wine, peppercorns, cream, mustard, eggs and a couple of shakes of hot pepper sauce to taste. Process for 30-40 seconds until the leeks are roughly chopped.
 Place a spoonful of the chopped leek mixture in the bottom of the greased loaf tin, arrange the four whole leeks on top and pour over the balance of the mixture. Cover the tin with foil and place it in a *bain-marie*, or a deep baking tray with enough boiling water to reach halfway up the tin. Place in the oven and bake for 45-50 minutes until set.
 To make the vinaigrette, place all the ingredients in a jar with a screwtop lid and shake vigorously until mixed.
 Remove the terrine from the oven and allow to cool. Unmould it by running a knife round the edges then cut into slices using a very sharp knife. Serve warm or cold, garnished with whole chives and accompanied by the vinaigrette.

Honeyed Ricotta *with* Fruit Crudités

Ricotta cheese is an excellent vehicle for the heady, almost almondy sweetness of orange blossom honey. Served with exotic, or any kind of fresh fruits, it makes a healthy, nutritious snack or an adventurous starter. It is also good spread on crackers or savoury biscuits.

SERVES 4

- 500g • 1lb ricotta cheese
- 3tbsp orange blossom honey
- 1 papaya
- 1 honeydew melon
- 1 mango

Mix the ricotta cheese and honey in a large bowl until well blended. Spoon the mixture into four 120ml/4fl oz heart-shaped perforated moulds lined with muslin or paper towel. Press the ricotta down gently then place on a tray to catch moisture from the ricotta. Chill in the refrigerator for 1-2 hours.
 Meanwhile, cut the skin off the papaya, melon and mango. Slice into thin strips lengthways.
 To unmould, take the muslin or paper towel and lift out of the moulds. Turn out the shaped ricottas onto individual plates and surround each with strips of fruit.

First Courses

First Courses

Wholewheat Pancakes *with* Honey *and* Crispy Bacon

Topped with whipped butter and piping hot crispy bacon, this scrumptious American-style snack is made with honey reflecting the North American love of mixing sweet and savoury. It is perfect for brunch or a light meal.

SERVES 4

150g/5oz stoneground wholemeal flour
pinch salt
300ml • ½pt full cream milk
1 size 2 egg
2tsp acacia honey, warmed

Topping
90g • 3oz salted butter, at room temperature
1tsp single cream
8 rashers streaky bacon
1tbsp acacia honey

Put the flour into a large bowl and make a well in the centre with a spoon. Sprinkle in a good pinch of salt.

Pour the milk into another bowl, add the egg and whisk together until well mixed. Drizzle the warmed honey into the egg mixture, whisking constantly.

Pour half of the egg mixture into the well in the flour and, using a fork, whisk the liquid gently without touching the flour; this allows small amounts of flour to slip into the liquid from the sides without forming any lumps. Continue whisking until the pancake batter is smooth.

Add the rest of the egg mixture, whisking quickly with the fork. Set the batter aside until needed.

For the topping, place the butter and the cream in a bowl and whisk with an electric beater or by hand until creamy and light. Leave at room temperature until needed.

Place a frying pan over a medium to high heat, add the bacon rashers and fry for 8-10 minutes until the bacon is crispy and all the milky liquid has evaporated.

Meanwhile, heat a crêpe pan or small nonstick frying pan until hot. If you do not have either of these, use an ordinary frying pan with some butter. Cook the pancakes one at a time using about 90ml/3fl oz of the batter for each pancake. Cook on one side for about 1 minute and when the batter begins to form small bubbles turn the pancake using an egg flip or spatula. Cook the other side for 1 minute until browned. Place each cooked pancake on a warmed serving plate.

To serve, drizzle 1 teaspoon of honey over each pancake, add a dollop of whipped butter and 2 rashers of crispy bacon.

Cinnamon *and* Honey French Toast

French toast is a clever way of transforming stale bread into something delectable. The addition of honey makes it even more delicious – perfect for a leisurely brunch or a self-indulgent snack at any time of the day.

SERVES 4

8 slices stale white bread
4tbsp clear honey
2 size 2 eggs
300ml • ½pt full cream milk
60g • 2oz salted butter
2tsp ground cinnamon

Spread one side of each slice of bread with 1 teaspoon of honey and leave it for a few minutes to soak into the bread. In a large flat casserole dish, whisk the eggs with 1½ tablespoons of the honey with a fork until blended. Add the milk, beating for another minute or so.

Melt the butter and 2 teaspoons of honey in a large flat-based frying pan; keep the frying pan over a very low heat until the bread is ready to be cooked.

Dip one slice of bread at a time in the egg mixture allowing it to absorb the liquid for 8-10 seconds; do not let it get too soggy though or it will fall apart.

Turn the heat under the frying pan up to high. When it is hot put in 2 slices of bread and cook for 2-3 minutes on each side until golden brown; cooking only 2 slices at a time prevents the bread from sticking together in an overcrowded pan.

Sprinkle each slice with ¼ teaspoon of cinnamon and serve warm.

Sweetness and Light

"Instead of dirt and poison we have rather chosen to fill our hives with honey and wax; thus furnishing mankind with the two noblest things, which are sweetness and light."

The Battle of the Books, Jonathan Swift, 1667–1745

This ceramic box has been designed to resemble a honeycomb – the bees make delightful motifs.

Prosciutto *and* Aubergine Crostini

The topping for these crostini (Italian toasted bread) is inspired by the ancient Roman practice of glazing ham with honey. Prosciutto is an intensely flavoured Italian cured ham, and the use of rosemary honey reinforces the Mediterranean origin of the dish. Ciabatta, a flattish Italian bread, is available from many supermarkets and bakeries, but other white breads could be substituted.

MAKES 12

1 aubergine
175ml • 6fl oz olive oil
4tbsp roughly chopped fresh oregano plus torn leaves for garnish
2 large cloves garlic, crushed
1 ciabatta loaf
2tsp rosemary honey
12 rashers bacon (about 300g • 10oz)

Preheat the oven to 220°C/425°F/gas mark 7.

Slice the aubergine into 24 1cm/½in thick discs and place them on a baking tray. Brush them liberally with olive oil on both sides. Sprinkle half of the chopped oregano over the slices. Place them in the oven and bake for 20 minutes until they begin to brown. Turn them, sprinkle with the remaining chopped oregano and bake for a further 5 minutes. Keep warm.

Cut the ciabatta bread into 12 1cm/½in thick slices and place them on another baking tray. Spread both sides with oil, then smear the top surface with half of the crushed garlic. Bake in the oven for 10 minutes until golden brown and crisp. Turn the slices over, smear them with the remainder of the garlic and bake for a further 5 minutes.

Meanwhile, warm 1 tablespoon of olive oil with the honey in a frying pan. Toss in the rashers of prosciutto and cook for 5-6 minutes until curling and slightly crisp.

To assemble the crostini, place 2 aubergine discs side by side on each slice of baked bread, top with a curl of prosciutto and garnish with oregano leaves.

Honey in Myth and Legend

Myths and legends about honey and bees are widespread throughout the world, and to some extent they still colour the way we view the golden liquid and the insects which produce it.

By their very nature, legends are impossible to date, but the origins of many old tales must come from the earliest times of honey gathering. One of the enduring myths which was found in many cultures was that of honey signifying "truth". The Hebrew for bee is *dbure*, meaning word, so the bee has a mission to bring the Divine Word or truth. If, as was supposed, a bee alighted on the lips of Plato and St Ambrose when they were children, then these men were sure to be blessed with truth and genius. Honey was put on new-born babies' lips in the hope of endowing them with wisdom and happiness – a custom which was followed in places as far apart as the Ivory Coast of Africa, Germany and India. The Egyptians, too, saw honey as imparting this gift of truth, eating it at certain festivals and incanting "Sweet is the Truth" as they did so.

The ancient Greeks believed that honey was the first food, pre-dating even the creation of the world. It was therefore seen as the food of the gods. The mighty god Zeus was brought up secretly in a cave by nursemaids, after his mother Rhea gave birth to him. The nursemaids, Amalthea and Melissa, fed him on milk and honey. (The name Melissa means "she who makes honey".) The Greeks also had their own patron-god of bees and beekeepers, named Aristaeus. This Arcadian shepherd was the son of Apollo and came from the island of Malta, once known as Melita, or island of honey. The legend of Aristaeus led to the belief that bees spontaneously generate – a view held until at least the seventeenth century, when scientists were able to explain the life cycle of the bee. The story tells how Aristaeus was deprived of his beloved bees after causing the deaths of the woman he loved and her husband. He made sacrifices, including four bulls, to atone for these deaths and after several days "huge and trailing clouds of bees, that now in the treetops unite and hang like a bunch of grapes from the pliant branches" were seen coming from the animals.

There are many myths worldwide about the origins of bees. People could not understand how new bees were formed, never seeing the insects mate and not understanding that just one bee, the queen, was responsible for a whole colony of insects. In the Byzantine civilisation, bees were thought to be the reincarnations of souls of the dead who had returned to earth and were therefore revered, while the Maya Indians from Central America believed that the insects came from some wondrous hive in the centre of the earth and flew from it like sparks spilling from a volcano.

Telling the bees

Even in more modern times, it was believed that bees would thrive only in harmonious families, and in both England and North America they were supposed to be included in family happenings. They were considered to be models of domestic peace and harmony and were also highly industrious workers, attributes to which most households aspired. "Telling the bees" was vitally important, whether it was good or bad news or simply everyday happenings. Bees had to be told of a death in the family or they would die too. The bad news had to be given before sunrise on the following day for all to be well.

Sometimes a piece of funeral cake and a drink of wine was left by the hive after a funeral. The bees might also be formally invited to the funeral, or the beehives turned round as the coffin was carried out of the house past them; this was a practice commonly followed in Devon and observed in the eighteenth century. Country people, believing that the bees took part in seasonal feasts, gave them extra honey or sugar on New Year's Day and strewed salt as a general protection for the insects on Good Friday.

The tradition of passing on family news to the bees is evoked in this country rhyme:
Marriage, birth or burying
News across the seas,
All your sad or marrying
You must tell the bees.

This painting, entitled Venus with Cupid the Honey Thief, *by Lucas Cranach the Elder, shows a juvenile Cupid taking honeycomb oblivious to the bees around him. Cupid was the son of Venus and Mercury.*

The ancient Greeks found honey to be soporific. According to legend Zeus gave his father a honey drink before tying him up and de-throning him.

The Honeymoon Period

A honeymoon, or honeymonth, was traditionally the month spent after a wedding, although it has now come to mean a special break taken by a couple after their marriage. Whether it simply signified a sweet and happy first month, or whether it was connected to actual rituals involving honey, is not clear. Many cultures used honey as part of the wedding ceremony. Hindu newlyweds were sometimes married in the presence of a bowl of honey and as the groom kissed the bride he would say to her "honey, this is honey, the speech of thy tongue is honey, in my mouth lives the honey of the bee, in my teeth lives peace".

CHAPTER TWO

MAIN COURSES

In almost every cuisine, there are main course recipes that show off the perfect marriage of sweet honey and savoury meats. The honey is often used alongside fruits, spices and herbs in such mouthwatering dishes as tagine of chicken and apricots or sweet honey-glazed rack of lamb infused with the perfume of thyme.

Main Courses

Honey has always held an important place in culinary history and modern life is becoming increasingly a rediscovery of the past. Honey-cured hams or glossy baked gammon coated with honey and mustard are a throwback to medieval times, invoking images of banquets and suckling pigs. Many a medieval cook reached out for these alluring condiments to dress up an ageing and tired joint of meat. From its prominent place in the kitchen and brewhouse, honey found its way into main course dishes such as duck or ham, its sweetness mingling with the salty, sharp and spicy flavours of ancient preservatives. Recipes using a combination of honey and fish, meat or poultry can sometimes have a cloying oversweetness, but this is countered particularly well by the sharpness of citrus fruits or the sourness of cherries or plums.

The Fishwife, *Adriaen van Ostrade, 1672*

Swarm

"A swarm of bees in May
Is worth a cow and a calf
that day;
A swarm of bees in June
Is worth a silver spoon;
A swarm of bees in July
Is not worth a butterfly."

TRADITIONAL IRISH
RHYME

WARM DUCK BREAST *with* MOROCCAN HONEY SAUCE

Inspired by the Moroccan fondness for honey, this exotically spiced crisp-skinned duck is perfectly matched by Couscous with Pistachios and Currants (page 80).

SERVES 4

1 cinnamon stick, halved
1tbsp strong hot black coffee
¼tsp ground allspice
¼tsp ground nutmeg
4¼tbsp chestnut honey

2tsp sugar
4 duck breasts with skin
125g • 4oz butter
300ml • ½pt duck or chicken stock

Place 1 piece of cinnamon stick in a shallow bowl, pour the hot coffee over and leave for 15 minutes to infuse. Remove the cinnamon stick and discard.

Place the allspice, nutmeg, cloves, 2 teaspoons of the honey and sugar in a small bowl. Pour in the coffee and stir well to mix. Brush the mixture on to the skin of the duck breasts and leave for 2-3 hours to marinate. Set the remainder of the spiced marinade aside for the sauce.

Heat a heavy-based saucepan over a high heat until very hot. Place the marinated duck breasts in the pan, skin side down, and pan-fry for 5 minutes. Turn the breasts over and pan-fry for 2-3 minutes then transfer to a baking tray. Keep warm.

To make the sauce, pour all but 2 teaspoons of the duck fat from the pan. Add the butter. When this has melted, add the remainder of the marinade and pour in the stock. Add the remaining half of the cinnamon stick and the remaining honey. Simmer the liquid for about 8-10 minutes until it is reduced and clings to the back of a spoon. Remove the cinnamon stick and discard.

To serve, slice the duck breast into 5mm/2in thick slices, arrange on large plates and spoon the sauce over them.

Honeyed Gammon *with a* Herb Crust

This succulent shoulder of gammon seasoned with honey and covered with a herb crust is based on the way the Romans would have cooked their ham in Classical times. Try it as an evening meal with roast vegetables or simply served with crusty bread and the mustard of your choice.

SERVES 4–6

1.5kg • 3lb unsmoked shoulder of gammon, tied
6 cloves
¼tsp black peppercorns
¼tsp green peppercorns
3tbsp rosemary honey
2 bay leaves
2 sprigs parsley plus 1tbsp roughly chopped
1 sprig fresh rosemary plus 1tsp roughly chopped
1 sprig fresh thyme plus ½tsp roughly chopped
90g • 3oz fresh brown breadcrumbs
1tbsp butter, melted
freshly ground black pepper

Place the gammon in a large saucepan with the cloves, peppercorns and 1 tablespoon of honey. Make a bunch of bouquet garni by tying together the bay leaves and the sprigs of parsley, rosemary and thyme with string then put the bouquet garni in the saucepan and cover with water. Bring the water to the boil and simmer for 45 minutes. Preheat the oven to 190°C/375°F/gas mark 5.

To make the herb crust put the chopped parsley, rosemary and thyme with the breadcrumbs in a bowl and add 1 tablespoon of honey and the melted butter. Stir until mixed, then season with the black pepper and set aside until the gammon is cooked.

Drain the gammon and place it in a baking tray, allowing it to cool slightly before snipping the string. Remove the layer of fat from the top of the gammon then with a sharp knife make four incisions downwards into the gammon about 2.5cm • 1 inch wide until the knife nearly reaches the base of the gammon but doesn't cut through the bottom.

Place 1 teaspoon of honey in each incision, then press the crust firmly onto the ham until it is totally covered. Bake in the oven for 30 minutes until the crust is browned. Carve into slices with a sharp knife.

Thai Sweet *and* Sour Fish

Baked whole, the succulent flesh of the fish is permeated with the flavours of the honey marinade; the process is assisted by three slits on each side of the fish. Honey is also used to flavour the accompanying chilli dipping sauce. Serve with plain boiled rice tossed with fresh coriander leaves and toasted cumin seeds.

SERVES 4

1 x 2kg • 4½lb whole red snapper, orange roughy or other whole white fish
2 x 7.5cm • 3in sticks lemon grass
3 cloves garlic, 2 crushed, 1 peeled
2.5cm • 1in piece fresh ginger root, peeled and grated
1 large red chilli pepper, roughly chopped
1 large green chilli pepper, roughly chopped
1 lime, juice only
2 x 2.5cm • 1in pieces coriander root and stalk, chopped
3½tbsp chopped fresh basil
1 small bunch coriander with roots
½tsp coarse sea salt
1½tsp crushed dried chilli seeds
4tbsp lime blossom honey
basil leaves for garnish

Preheat the oven to 190°C/375°F/gas mark 5.

Line a good-sized roasting pan with a piece of foil large enough to wrap round the fish. With a very sharp knife make three diagonal cuts along each side of the fish.

To make the marinade, first remove and discard the tough outer leaves of one of the lemon grass sticks. Finely chop and place in a bowl with the crushed garlic, ginger, chilli peppers, lime juice, chopped coriander root and basil. Mix them together well.

Place the crushed dried chilli seeds and honey in a bowl with 6 tablespoons of warm water and stir until the honey is dissolved. Put 6 tablespoons of the mixture into a small bowl as a dipping sauce for serving.

To flavour the fish, spoon half of the remaining sweet chilli sauce on to one side of the fish then rub in half of the marinade. Turn the fish and repeat the process. Place the remaining lemon grass stick, coriander and whole garlic clove in the cavity of the fish. Sprinkle the fish with the sea salt, fold the foil over the fish and seal.

Bake the fish in the oven for 15 minutes. Remove from the oven, undo the foil and baste the fish with a few spoonfuls of the sauce. Reseal, return the fish to the oven and bake for a further 10-15 minutes until cooked. The flesh should be bright white and flake away from the bone easily.

Serve on a large platter topped with basil leaves or cut each side of the fish into fillets and place, using a spatula, on individual plates. Serve accompanied by the sweet chilli dipping sauce.

Indonesian Satay Spare Ribs

The combination of fragrant spices, honey and peanuts gives this dish a real flavour of Indonesian food. The spare ribs can be served as finger food or as part of a sit-down meal garnished with coriander leaves and accompanied by Crunchy Almond Noodles (page 81).

SERVES 4

3 cloves garlic, crushed
2 shallots, finely chopped
1tsp ground cumin
1tsp ground coriander
½tsp ground turmeric
½tsp chilli powder
2tbsp ketjap manis (Indonesian soy sauce)
1tsp sambal olek (chilli purée)
1tbsp clear honey
2tbsp smooth peanut butter
1tbsp vegetable oil
1kg • 2lb pork spare ribs, on the bone
coriander leaves for garnish

In a bowl, mix the garlic, shallots, cumin, coriander, turmeric and chilli powder into a rough paste. Stir in the ketjap manis, sambal olek, honey and peanut butter until well blended, then stir in the vegetable oil with 1 tablespoon of water to thin the paste slightly.

Arrange the spare ribs in a large shallow casserole dish. Using a pastry brush or the back of a teaspoon spread the paste over them, turning them to completely cover. Place in the refrigerator and leave to marinate for at least 6 hours, or preferably overnight.

Heat a barbecue or grill until hot and cook the spare ribs for 20-25 minutes until crispy and well-browned, turning them every 5 minutes.

Allow to cool slightly if serving as a finger food.

Spicy Pineapple Baby Chicken

Lime blossom honey and pineapple juice lend sweet and fruity overtones to these eastern spiced baby chickens. Excellent for a barbecue, they can also form part of an oriental meal made up of Chinese Stir-Fried Vegetables (page 85) or Crunchy Almond Noodles (page 81). Or they can be served with freshly boiled white or brown rice into which 60m/2fl oz of the cooked marinade has been stirred.

SERVES 4

300ml • ½pt pure pineapple juice, unsweetened
100ml • 3½fl oz soy sauce
100ml • 3½fl oz rice wine
6 small dried chilli peppers, snipped
4tbsp lime blossom honey
4 baby chicken or poussin

Place all the ingredients except for the chicken in a large casserole dish and stir until well mixed. With a pair of poultry scissors or sharp knife cut the chicken in half down the backbone. Place in the refrigerator for 4-5 hours or overnight to marinate, turning the chicken halfway through.

Preheat the oven to 190°C/375°F/gas mark 5. Line a baking tray with a baking sheet or foil to prevent the marinade juices baking on to the tray.

Remove the chicken from the marinade and place on the baking tray. Bake in the oven for 30-35 minutes, basting occasionally with the marinade to improve the flavour and give a syrupy coating, until the chicken is cooked through and golden brown.

Crispy Loin *of* Pork *with* Plum *and* Orange Sauce

Following the centuries-old custom of flavouring pork and ham with honey, this succulent dish combines a traditional loin of pork with a contemporary sauce. The dish is also good served with Baked Honeyed Squash (page 78). If the plums are a bit tart, add an extra teaspoon of honey when you cook them.

SERVES 4

1.25kg • 2½lb boned loin of pork with fat, rolled and tied
4 fresh sage leaves
½tsp salt
SAUCE
75g • 2½oz salted butter
6 ripe plums (about 300g • 10oz), roughly chopped
2½tbsp orange blossom honey
250ml • 8fl oz freshly squeezed orange juice
250ml • 8fl oz port
1½tbsp plum jam
1tbsp fresh sage, torn then roughly chopped

Preheat the oven to 230°C/450°F/gas mark 8.

Place the pork in a roasting pan. Push two whole sage leaves into each end of the roll. Rub the salt into the skin of the pork. Roast in the oven for 20 minutes, turn the heat down to 200°C/400°F/gas mark 6 and roast for a further 40-45 minutes, or until the liquid runs clear when the pork is pierced with a skewer.

Meanwhile, make the sauce. Melt the butter in a heavy-based frying pan then add the plums and honey. Cook for 3-5 minutes until the plums are beginning to soften.

Add the orange juice, port and plum jam, bring to the boil then reduce the heat and simmer for 25-30 minutes until the sauce is reduced to a syrupy consistency.

Remove the roast pork from the oven, slice off the crackling and return it to the oven to crisp up further. Allow the pork to rest for 5-8 minutes before carving.

Meanwhile, toss the chopped sage into the sauce and reheat gently.

Slice the pork into 5mm/¼in discs then cut these across to make half rounds. Overlap these on individual plates, spoon the reheated sauce over and garnish with crackling.

CANTONESE SHREDDED BEEF

Stir-frying over high heat cooks food quickly while sealing in all the flavour. In this recipe, the beef is cooked until crisp and sweet. The flowery orange blossom honey counteracts the spiciness of the peppers while harmonizing with the sweetness of the carrots. The dish is best served with plain boiled rice to absorb the honeyed juices.

SERVES 4

2½tbsp sesame oil
3 cloves garlic, chopped
12 baby carrots (about 375g • 12oz), cut into 5cm • 2in strips
1½tbsp soy sauce
6tbsp orange blossom honey
¾tsp chilli powder or cayenne pepper
500g • 1lb beef fillet, cut into thin strips 5cm • 2in long
¼tsp salt

In a wok or non-stick frying pan heat the oil until hot. Add the garlic and cook until it is just turning golden.

Add the carrots with 2 teaspoons of soy sauce, 1 tablespoon of honey and ¼ teaspoon of chilli powder or cayenne pepper and stir-fry for 2-3 minutes until the carrots are just starting to soften.

Add the beef with the remainder of the soy sauce, honey, chilli powder or cayenne pepper and the salt. Stir-fry for a further 5-7 minutes until the beef is a dark golden brown and slightly crispy and the carrots are caramelized. Serve immediately.

Orange Blossom

Honey made from orange blossom can lend a distinctive flavour to a recipe as in Crispy Loin of Pork (left), but oranges themselves also have a natural affinity with honey. The sugar that makes honey sweet highlights the zest of the orange. Traditionally orange complements honey in sweet dishes, such as baklava, the Greek honey spiced cake, and savoury ones such as duck, where the citric acid orange helps to counteract the natural fattiness of the bird.

Performing Bees

One of the most unusually sited beehives is the one positioned on the roof of the Paris Opéra. Established in 1984 by Jean Paucton, a backstage worker in charge of set furniture, the hive produces a strong-tasting honey some people find overpowering. This unique flavour is due to the huge range of flowers from which the Opéra bees gather their nectar. Free to roam all over Paris, they visit flowers on the boulevards and balconies, in the large open parks and even the Père-Lachaise cemetery. And since the city is usually several degrees warmer than the outlying rural areas, flowers bloom earlier and so the urban bees have a longer honey-making season. The fruits of their labours are on sale, at a premium price, in the souvenir shop of the Opéra itself, and at Fauchon (above), the prestigious Paris food store.

Another French institution to have a link with beehives is the Comédie-Française, the prestigious theatre company founded by Louis XIV in 1680. The beehive was felt to be an appropriate symbol for an acting troupe since it represents individual effort by the many for the good of the whole. This modern souvenir chocolate coin carrying the beehive was produced as a memento of the money thrown as tokens of appreciation at the traditionally unpaid actors early in the history of the company.

Main Courses

Racks *of* Lamb *with a* Thyme *and* Honey Glaze

The use of thyme honey in this recipe cleverly links a traditional method of glazing meat with the subtle flavouring of fresh herbs. The result is handsome enough for an elegant dinner and particularly well matched in flavour to the Shallot Confit on page 86. Leaving on any excess fat improves the flavour of the dish.

SERVES 4

4 racks of lamb, each with 4 cutlets (about 1kg • 2lb)
2 cloves garlic, halved
1tsp yellow mustard seeds
2tbsp thyme honey
1tbsp fresh thyme leaves, stripped from the stems
sprigs of thyme for garnish

Preheat the oven to 200°C/400°F/gas mark 6.

Lay the racks of lamb flat in a roasting pan with the bones touching the base and rub the flesh all over with the cut ends of the garlic cloves. Crush the garlic cloves and place in a bowl.

Using a pestle and mortar crush the mustard seeds until they are just split open. Add the split seeds with the honey to the garlic and stir well, mixing all the ingredients evenly.

Spread the mixture over the back of the racks of lamb then sprinkle with the thyme leaves. Place immediately in the oven and bake for 15 minutes to crisp up the fat. Turn the heat down to 175°C/350°F/gas mark 4 and roast for a further 20 minutes, or until the liquid runs clear when the lamb is pierced with a skewer.

Serve the racks whole, garnished with sprigs of thyme.

Peas & Honey

*"I eat my peas with honey,
I've done it all my life,
It makes my peas taste funny,
But it keeps them on my knife."*

ANON.

Main Courses

Chestnuts

Chestnut honey is made from the blossom of the sweet or Spanish chestnut, which is sometimes known in England as the "breadfruit tree" (not to be confused with the tropical breadfruit tree grown in the South Pacific) because it provides man with so much for free. The nuts can be eaten fresh in soups, casseroles, stuffings and pies, often bulking out scarce and expensive meat; they can be dried for use in cooking or ground to a flour for making breads and batters, or they may be candied. Even the leaves can be used as winter feed for cattle.

Tagine *of* Chicken *with* Apricots *and* Prunes

A tagine is a traditional Moroccan stew cooked very slowly in an earthenware pot (also called a tagine). This method of cooking allows the meat to absorb all the flavours. Chestnut honey contributes a rich, nutty sweetness to this chicken version which is emphasized by the honeyed apricots, although ordinary dried apricots will do. Serve the tagine on a bed of couscous to soak up the juices.

SERVES 4

30g • 1oz butter
3tbsp vegetable oil
2 cloves garlic
pinch saffron
¼tsp cayenne pepper
¼tsp finely ground black pepper
¼tsp crushed coriander seeds
¼tsp ground ginger

1.5kg • 3lb chicken, cut into 8 pieces
12 shallots, peeled
90g • 3oz honeyed dried apricots
125g • 4oz prunes
1tbsp chestnut honey
¼tsp ground cinnamon

Melt the butter in a large saucepan or casserole then add the oil and heat. Add the garlic, a good pinch of saffron, the cayenne pepper, black pepper, crushed coriander seeds and ginger and fry everything together for 1-2 minutes. Add the chicken pieces, toss them in the spice mixture to cover them well and cook for 3-4 minutes to allow the spices to penetrate.

Add sufficient water to the pan or casserole to almost cover the chicken. Bring to the boil then simmer for 45-50 minutes, covered. Add the shallots and cook for another 20 minutes, uncovered.

After 20 minutes, add the apricots, prunes, honey and cinnamon then continue to cook for 30 minutes until the sauce has reduced and the chicken is almost falling off the bone. The dish can be served immediately, but its rich flavours will improve if it is made in advance and stored, covered, in the refrigerator for a couple of days.

Brewing Honey

Mead and metheglin are both fermented honey-based drinks, the difference between them being that mead simply consists of fermented honey and water with no additional flavourings, while metheglin is flavoured with spices and sometimes herbs. It is not uncommon, though, to come across versions that do not conform to this purist distinction. Mead has been brewed worldwide since very early times, and, according to legend, was drunk by Dionysius and Bacchus before the vine was cultivated. Records show that mead had become popular in England by 334 BC, and it remained a staple drink in England and other northern European countries until the nineteenth century, when a decline in bee numbers led to an increase in the price of honey. But mead continued to be brewed on a small scale, and is still produced today.

Old Sussex Recipe *for* Mead

Take 6 pounds of any light floral honey and put it into a big pot with 16 pints of water, rainwater if possible, and heat until boiling. Add spices you like best such as cinnamon, ginger, cloves or nutmeg. Then reduce over a gentle heat until only 6 pints of liquid remain. Pour the liquid into pottery or earthenware pots and allow to cool. Add about 1 ounce of fresh yeast and leave to ferment for 3 days. When fermentation is over pour into casks, or bottles, and keep for a year before drinking.

Queen Elizabeth's Metheglin

First, gather a bushel of sweetbriar leaves, and a bushel of thyme, half a bushel of rosemary, and a peck of bay leaves. Seethe all these, being well-washed, in a furnace not less than 120 gallons, of fair water. Let them boil the space of half an hour or better, and then pour out all the water and herbs into a vat. Let it stand until it be but milk warm, then strain the water from the herbs, and take to every six gallons of water, one gallon of the finest honey, and put it into the boorne. Labour it together half an hour, then let it stand for two days, stirring it well twice or thrice each day. Then take the liquor and boil it anew, and when it does seethe, skim it as long as there remains any dross. When it is clear, put it into a vat as before, and there let it be cooled. You must then have in readiness a kive of new ale or beer, which as soon as you have emptied, suddenly whelm it upside down, and set it up again, and presently put in the metheglin, and let it stand three days a-working. And then turn it up in barrels, tying at every taphole (by a pack thread) a little bag of beaten cloves and mace, to the value of an ounce. Leave for half a year before drinking.

Strong Honey Ale

Honey can also be added to hop-based brews. As well as reducing the bitterness of the hops, the flavour of the honey adds a unique roundness. This ale can be very strong, and should only be drunk in moderation!

MAKES 5 LITRES (1 GALLON)
550g • 20oz pure malt extract
300g • 10oz clear honey
30g • 1¼oz Goldings hops
350ml • 12fl oz pure apple juice
1 sachet ale yeast

YOU WILL ALSO NEED: Chempro SDP or solution of sodium metabisulphite; large plastic container with lid (holding at least 10 litres/1½ gallon) for fermenting; long plastic spoon or spatula; wine or beer hydrometer; plastic bottles.

Put about 1 litre (2 pints) of cold water in a large stainless steel pan over a medium heat. Stir in the malt extract, honey and apple juice using a plastic spoon or spatula. Bring to the boil and add 25g (1oz) of the hops to this mixture. Stir well, cover partially and boil steadily but not too vigorously for 45 minutes, stirring occasionally to beat back the hops. After 45 minutes, stir in the remaining 5g (¼oz) of hops and boil steadily for another 15–20 minutes. Turn off the heat.

Sterilize the large plastic container, the lid and the plastic spoon or spatula, rinse carefully with cold water and drain. Now strain the liquid into the fermenting vessel and top it up with cold water to 5 litres (1 gallon). Stir vigorously to aerate, cover and cool to room temperature. When cool, add the contents of the yeast sachet, cover and store in a warm place until fermentation is complete. Check this by measuring the specific gravity with a sterilized hydrometer until the reading stays constant for a couple of days. Fermentation takes from 3 to 5 days.

When fermentation is complete, sterilize, rinse and drain the required number of bottles and tops. Fill each bottle to within about 50mm (2 inches) of the top and seal. Store the bottles in a warm place for about 5 days. Check that not too much pressure is building up in the bottles and unscrew the tops to release excess pressure if necessary, sealing them up again. After 5 days, move the bottles to a cool, dark place and leave to mature for at least 3 months. When ready, decant the ale into another container before drinking, taking care not to disturb the yeast sediment.

Honey Pots

While honey's main culinary purpose in the past was as an ingredient for cooking and brewing, it is more likely to appear on today's table as a spread or sweetener for cereals or puddings. Afternoon tea may be on the decline, with fewer occasions to spread honey on slices of fresh bread and butter, toasted muffins or crumpets, but we still buy plenty of the stuff and many of us decant it from its jar into a special honey pot. In the Victorian and Edwardian days of long, leisurely breakfasts and teas served by the fire in the drawing room it was commonplace to have a choice of home-made jams, savoury spreads, marmalades and honeys. Silver, china or cut-glass pots and jars were specially made to hold the many different flavours of jam and honey.

Honey pots have always captured the imagination of designers, given that the world of bees, hives and honeycombs offer so many wonderful visual references to inspire them. The skep and hive were favourite shapes to make into pots – complete with lids, of course, and a space to hold a spoon or special honey drizzler. Honey might be poured from its original jar into the decorative one or, if the decorative container was large enough and the right shape, a complete jar of honey could be stood inside it. Special honey spoons were marketed with a little hook half way up their stem. After using it to put honey on your slice of bread, the spoon was hooked over the jar edge to drain. Why this was seen as necessary is a slight mystery, but it was presumably to save the risk of sticky fingers if the spoon slipped lower into the liquid honey. The 1930s and 1950s saw a rise in the popularity of inexpensive, novelty tea sets and other china, which were often elaborately moulded and highly decorated. Honey pots were a favourite choice for mass production, especially to be sold as souvenirs. Tea-time was still an important family meal; for many it was the main meal of the day. It included a hot dish followed by bread and butter and cakes, washed down with tea. A quirky china honey pot was just the thing to brighten up the table.

1. *This Roman honey jar is made from glazed clay. Presumably parchment or skin would have been tied over the top if the honey was to have been stored for any length of time. The handles made it easy to carry as honey was an important sacrifice to various gods and had to be transported to temples and shrines.*

2. *This elaborate and ornate ink stand takes the bee hive as its design starting point. Made from ormolu and bronze the four lotus shapes around the hive are for holding pens.*

4. This china honey pot is a slightly unusual shape but still appears to be based on a straw skep. It has a stand and lid decorated with large moulded leaves and dates from around 1730.

3. The bee skep shape was the most obvious and enduring inspiration for honey pot makers. This one made from glass was originally decorated but the colour has worn away with constant use.

5. This honey pot is made from Faience and dates from the eighteenth century. Peasant pottery of this type is generally brightly decorated in this bold style and the blue, green and yellow design showing a woman picking flowers is very typical.

6. This pale yellow glass honey pot was made in Somerset between 1830 and 1840. It is easy to imagine it on a gracious early Victorian tea table amongst fine bone china tea services and elegant silver.

7. These mass-produced ceramic pots from the 1950s are in the chunky style typical of the decade. The images used, of a skep and a honeycomb, are perennially popular.

8. One of a pair of small but highly detailed English silver honey pots and stands which date from the time of George III based on a straw skep shape.

9. This honey jar, from Boyne Valley Honey, continues the tradition of honey containers resembling beehives, whilst providing modern convenience.

CHAPTER THREE

VEGETABLES

A hint of honey can do surprising things for everyday and more unusual vegetables and accompaniments, from rich wintry spiced red cabbage to light fluffy couscous studded with nuts and dried fruit. Root vegetables, no matter how sweet they are, always benefit from a touch of honey as well.

VEGETABLES

Vegetables are an integral part of a meal, so why treat them as an afterthought? Many have a sweetish tinge, which is enhanced by a little honey. But take care not to smother their natural sweetness with overpowering flavours. More robust vegetables, like squash or fennel, cope well with unusual or powerful flavours. Their vast range of textures and colours make vegetables ideal for exciting stir-fry dishes, perhaps combined with honey, ginger and plenty of garlic. Rice, the staple diet of most of the world, and other grains have a natural blandness which is transformed magically by subtle blends of herbs, spices and honey. Honey is also perfect for fruit or vegetable confits, with their combination of sweet and sour flavours. With the increasing availability of exciting and exotic vegetables from all over the world and a growing trend towards meals based around vegetables and pulses, these recipes represent many styles and cultures, both classic and innovative.

Fresco of a vegetable market from Issogno Castle, Valle Aosta, Italy, fifteenth century

Red Cabbage Tossed *in* Honey *and* Caraway

Adapted from traditional German recipes for red cabbage, this version is made sweeter by the addition of honey. Balsamic vinegar, a mild, intensely fragrant wine vinegar, is kinder to the honey than a more traditional, harsher type would be. The dish goes well with Crispy Loin of Pork (page 64). Caraway seeds can be toasted by stirring them around a hot frying pan for about 1 minute.

SERVES 4

1 red cabbage (about 500g • 1lb)
75g • 2½oz salted butter
1 onion, sliced
60g • 2oz sultanas
1½tbsp clover honey
1tbsp balsamic vinegar or other red wine vinegar
½tsp caraway seeds, toasted

Using a large, sharp knife cut the cabbage into 5mm/⅕in shreds. In a large saucepan, melt the butter and sauté the onion over a medium heat for 2-3 minutes until transparent.

Add the sultanas to the pan and toss through the butter. Stir in the honey, mixing well. Add the shredded cabbage and the balsamic vinegar. Stir in the toasted caraway seeds until mixed through.

Turn the heat down to low, cover and steam the red cabbage for 10-15 minutes until it is tender, tossing once or twice with tongs during the cooking time. Serve immediately.

Baked Honeyed Squash

This caramelized squash melts in the mouth and makes a scrumptious accompaniment to poultry and meat dishes. It is especially good with Racks of Lamb with a Thyme and Honey Glaze (page 67). If you cannot find butternut squash, substitute any other orange squash or pumpkin.

SERVES 4

500g • 1lb butternut squash, deseeded
30g • 1oz salted butter
1tbsp creamy honey, warmed
½tsp chopped fresh rosemary, or ¼tsp dried rosemary

Preheat the oven to 190°C/375°F/gas mark 5.

Cut the squash into 5mm/¼in rounds and cut these in half to make half circles. Place the squash pieces in a bowl with the warmed honey and toss to coat well.

Arrange the squash, overlapping the pieces, in a roasting pan or large shallow ovenproof dish. Drizzle the honey syrup left in the bowl over the squash. Dot the squash with the butter then sprinkle with the rosemary.

Bake in the oven for 30-35 minutes until golden brown and caramelized.

Sing a Song of Sixpence

*"The king was in his counting-house
Counting out his money
The queen was in the parlour
Eating bread and honey."*

TRADITIONAL NURSERY RHYME

Vegetables

Couscous *with* Pistachios *and* Currants

Any spiced meat or poultry would be enhanced by this sweet, nutty variation of the classic Moroccan couscous. It is particularly good as an accompaniment to Warm Duck Breast with Moroccan Sauce (page 60).

SERVES 4

300g • 10oz couscous
90g • 3oz butter
90g • 3oz pistachios, shelled
45g • 1½oz currants
1¾tbsp lime blossom honey

Place the couscous in a large bowl and pour over 250ml/8fl oz boiling water. Stir thoroughly and leave for about 5 minutes to allow the grains to absorb the water and swell.

Melt the butter in a large frying pan then add the pistachios and currants. Cook for 2 minutes until the nuts begin to crispen, then add the honey and cook for a further 1-2 minutes. Add the soaked couscous and stir through for 2-3 minutes until well mixed and coated with butter and honey.

Crunchy Almond Noodles

Although honey is not often used in Chinese cuisine, the inclusion of fragrant orange blossom honey in this recipe introduces a pleasing sweet element to a traditional dish. Noodles are one of the staples of Far Eastern cooking; there, they are eaten at least once a day.

SERVES 4

60g • 2oz flaked almonds
180g • 6oz Chinese thread egg noodles
2tbsp sesame oil
1tbsp thick soy sauce
2tbsp orange blossom honey
10g • ⅓oz chives, snipped into 5cm • 2in lengths

Preheat the oven to 200°C/400°F/gas mark 6.

Put the flaked almonds on to a baking tray and place them in the oven for 3-5 minutes until golden. Remove and allow to cool.

Cook the noodles in a saucepan of boiling water, then drain. Pour the sesame oil and soy sauce into the same saucepan and add the honey. Return the noodles to the saucepan and toss gently to coat them evenly. Add the snipped chives and toss again. Finally, add the almonds, toss through and serve immediately.

If you work quickly during the last stages of preparation, the noodles should retain their heat; should you need to reheat them, either set the saucepan over a very low heat or place the noodles in the microwave on high for 30-40 seconds.

Vegetables

V E G E T A B L E S

GINGERED HONEY CARROTS

Sweet, honeyed carrots flavoured with the distinctive taste of freshly toasted cumin seeds take only a little more time to prepare than ordinary steamed carrots but have double the flavour. Cumin seeds can be toasted by stirring them around a hot frying pan for about 1 minute.

SERVES 4

60g • 2oz butter
8 carrots (about 500g • 1lb), cut into batons about 7.5cm • 3in long by 5mm • ¼in wide
5cm • 2in piece fresh root ginger, peeled and cut into thin strips
1tbsp acacia honey
½tsp cumin seeds, toasted

Melt the butter in a large frying pan, add the carrots and the ginger and sauté for 2-3 minutes.
　Add the honey and cook for a further 4-5 minutes until the carrots are tender but still firm. Add the toasted cumin seeds, toss thoroughly and warm through for 1 minute before serving.

Honey Lovers

Before man created purpose-built hives, bears developed various strategies to rob bees of their precious honey, such as waiting until night before knocking down a hive suspended from the underside of a rock. In the darkness, the bees tended to buzz around the site of the comb rather than attack the marauder.

Nowadays bears must adapt their honey-hunting skills to cope with man-made hives, sometimes protected in apiaries by an electric fence.

Baked Honey Beetroot

The unique flavour of beetroot is superbly matched by the sweetness of honey. Because it is cooked in an oven, this dish makes an ideal accompaniment for roast meats.

SERVES 4

1tbsp creamy honey
1tsp olive oil
8 baby beetroot (about 400g • 13oz), uncooked
¼tsp finely ground black pepper

Preheat the oven to 190°C/375°F/gas mark 5.

In a bowl large enough to hold all the beetroot, mix together the honey and the oil until blended.

Peel each beetroot and place in the bowl with the honey mixture. Toss the beetroot in the honey mixture then sprinkle with black pepper.

Place the beetroot in a casserole dish and drizzle any excess honey mixture over them. Bake in the oven for 35-40 minutes, turning the beetroots twice during the cooking time.

Chinese Stir-Fried Vegetables *with* Honey *and* Sesame Seeds

Honey and sesame seeds enhance the natural flavours of the crisp, stir-fried vegetables. The principle of stir-frying is to allow food to be cooked quickly before it loses any of its goodness or taste; a wok is specially shaped for this style of cooking, but a heavy-bottomed frying pan will do.

SERVES 4

- 2tbsp sesame oil
- 2 cloves garlic, roughly chopped
- 1 yellow sweet pepper, cut into thin strips
- 8 spring onions, cut on the diagonal into 2.5cm • 1in strips
- 150g • 5oz sugar snap peas
- 180g • 6oz bean sprouts
- 200g • 7oz pak choi (Chinese cabbage), trimmed, leaves left whole
- 1½tbsp sesame seeds
- 1½tbsp soy sauce
- 1½tbsp acacia honey

In a wok or heavy-bottomed frying pan heat the sesame oil over medium-high heat. When it is hot, add the garlic and sweet pepper and stir-fry until the pepper just begins to brown around the edges.

Add the spring onions and sugar snap peas and stir-fry for 1-2 minutes.

Add the bean sprouts, pak choi, sesame seeds, soy sauce and honey and stir-fry for a further 2-3 minutes. Serve immediately.

Shallot Confit

With the consistency of a chutney or marmalade, this confit is superb with meats and strong cheeses. The confit can be eaten warm; alternatively, it can be kept in a sealed jar in the refrigerator for up to one week and eaten cold.

SERVES 4

20 shallots (about 500g • 1lb), peeled
1 leek, sliced
100g • 4oz raisins
4tbsp white wine vinegar
2½tbsp clear honey
2½tbsp olive oil

Combine all the ingredients in a small saucepan. Place over a medium heat and bring to the boil.

Simmer over a low heat for 1¼ hours, or until the liquid has reduced and thickened to become syrupy. Keep a watchful eye on the heat during the simmering; if the heat is too high the syrup may burn. Allow the confit to cool slightly before serving.

Try shallot confit with Stilton or Roquefort cheese, or some cold slices of rare beef or lamb for a Mediterranean-style ploughman's lunch.

V E G E T A B L E S

This illustration, taken from Graphic Illustrations of Animals, Showing their Utility to Man, *beautifully illustrates the myriad and varied benefits we gain from the bee. In the form of honey it provides a basic food stuff and a medical remedy (1 and 5), while beeswax gives us light in the form of candles (3 and 4). Certain species of animals and birds rely on honey as a food source; here African tribemen follow ratels in order to locate honey for themselves (6). Other, more marginal benefits come in the form of wax flowers and wax museums (8 and 9). And from this picture (7) it would appear that bees have even been used as a weapon of war! However, we have a particular reason to be seriously grateful to the honey bee (2 and 10). It has been calculated that if bees were to become extinct, not only garden flowers but world crops would fail through lack of pollination. Deprived of food sources, we would not survive for more than two years.*

Wax Chandler.

For Light.

Queen. Drone. Europe Worker.

Honey Guide and Ratels.

Medicinal.

CHAPTER FOUR

Desserts

Because honey blends so perfectly with so many fresh and dried fruits, its inclusion can make fruit-based desserts even more delectable. It makes smooth and creamy puddings even more alluring and its hints of flower fragrances and mild sweetness enhance delicious delicate desserts, such as mousses and syllabubs.

Desserts

Ambrosia was the original food of the gods and we still use the word ambrosial for foods, particularly puddings, that are so delicious they hint at the divine. Honey really excels when it comes to desserts. More intensely sweet than the equivalent amount of sugar, it makes an ideal sweetening agent; whether liquid or set, it mixes easily and quickly with other ingredients.

Perfect in dishes including cream and yoghurt which will not be heated, it leaves no gritty texture as sugar would. And, as well as sweetness, it provides its own unique flavour, experienced at its best in simple dishes. Try thick Greek yoghurt drizzled with a dark, powerfully scented honey such as Greek mountain honey for a perfect marriage of flavours.

La Pâtisserie Gloppe aux Champs Elysées, *Jean Beraud, 1889*

Lavender Honey Cheesecake

Flavoured with lavender flowers and lavender honey, this delicious cheesecake evokes a hot, peaceful summer's day full of the sound of bees buzzing over clumps of heady blossom. If you use dried lavender, make sure they are organically dried and contain no colouring agents. You can decorate the cheesecake with crystallized lavender stems: dip stems in egg white then immediately in caster sugar, and place them on a wire cooling rack to dry.

SERVES 6-8

250g • 8oz shortbread biscuits
75g • 2½oz butter, melted
3tbsp lavender petals, fresh or dried, tied in muslin
180g • 6oz lavender honey
250g • 8oz light soft cheese
300ml • ½pt double cream

For the base, place the shortbread biscuits in a plastic bag and crush them using a rolling pin until quite fine. Place the biscuit crumbs in a bowl and stir in the melted butter. Press this mixture into a 23cm/9¼in diameter springform tin using the back of a large metal spoon and place in the refrigerator for 1 hour.

To make the lavender infusion, pour 2½ tablespoons of boiling water into a small bowl with 2 teaspoons of the lavender honey. Place the muslin sachet of lavender petals in the bowl and leave for 15 minutes to infuse. Remove the sachet and let the water cool.

In a large bowl, beat together the light soft cheese and the remainder of the honey until smooth then gradually add the lavender water until absorbed and the mixture is light and smooth. Whip the double cream until it forms soft peaks and gently fold into the soft cheese mixture. Pour the filling over the biscuit base then place in the refrigerator for 3-4 hours until set.

Before serving the cheesecake, run a warm knife round the edge of the springform tin. Serve cut into slices.

D E S S E R T S

Toffeed Apples *with* Honey Ice-cream

This delicious honey ice-cream made with fragrant heather honey, is quick and simple to prepare. It is quite divine served with caramelized apple.

SERVES 4

*2 crisp green eating apples
   (about 350g • 12oz)
2tbsp salted butter
2tbsp heather honey
7tbsp cognac*

Ice-cream
*2 size 2 eggs
4tbsp heather honey
600ml • 1pt double cream*

First make the ice cream. In a bowl beat together the eggs, honey and cream until well blended. Pour the mixture into a small saucepan and heat over a low heat stirring constantly until warm to the touch. Be careful not to overcook as the eggs will start to scramble if you do. Allow to cool.

Pour the ice-cream mixture into four 150ml/5fl oz moulds and place in the freezer for at least 3-4 hours until frozen solid.

Decore the apples and cut them into quarters, leaving the skins on. Slice the quarters wafer thin.

Melt the butter in a large frying pan, add the apples and sauté for 3-4 minutes. Add the honey and cognac and heat until bubbling. Continue to cook over a medium-high heat for 15-20 minutes until the mixture is a rich golden brown. Keep warm.

Remove the ice-cream from the moulds. Hold the base of each mould carefully under running cold water then run a knife round the edges to loosen the ice-cream. Turn out on to a large, flat dinner plate and allow to soften for 3-4 minutes. Spoon the warm toffed apples to one side and serve immediately.

Mrs Beeton

Mrs Beeton's Book of Household Management, *published in 1861, is recognized all over the world as an all-time cookery classic today. One of its most fascinating aspects is its insight into historical uses of and attitudes to food.*

At the time Mrs Beeton was writing, white sugar was the cheapest, and therefore the most popular, sweetening. However, she recognised the advantages of honey and used it for its preservative qualities: in a teabread so that it would keep well and to make a distinctively flavoured honey pudding. She also produced an orange marmalade that contained honey.

LIME *and* HONEY GRANITA

Like other sharp-tasting water ices, this granita can be used as a between-course palate cleanser or simply as a welcome refresher on a hot day. The lime honey complements the slightly tingling freshness of the champagne. The granita mixture can be kept for up to one week in an airtight container in the freezer.

SERVES 4

3 limes, chopped flesh and any juice plus zest for decoration
3½tbsp lime blossom honey
300ml • ½pt champagne or sparkling wine, at room temperature

Whisk the lime and the honey together in a bowl until they are well blended.

Pour the champagne or sparkling wine into the bowl, whisking constantly. When the honey is dissolved, pour the mixture into a shallow tin or tray that will not mark when scraped with a fork. Place in the freezer for 7-8 hours or overnight.

Remove the tin or tray from the freezer and, using a fork, crush the ice mixture to break it up. Place the granita in the freezer for at least 2-3 hours and serve decorated with lime zest.

HONEY *and* MADEIRA SYLLABUB

Syllabubs are old favourites, but this one has been given a new twist. Serve it straight from the refrigerator; if left standing at room temperature for too long, liquid will collect at the bottom of the glass or bowl. Beating the cream in a chilled bowl will thicken it and help it to hold its shape.

SERVES 4

400ml • 14fl oz double cream
2tbsp Canadian clover honey
160ml • 5½fl oz madeira
30g • 1oz flaked almonds
12 savioardi biscuits (Italian sponge finger biscuits)

Preheat the oven to 200°C/400°F/gas mark 6.

Place the cream in a chilled ceramic bowl or over ice and beat for 15-20 seconds until slightly thick.

Add the honey and beat for a further 10 seconds. Pour a continuous stream of madeira into the cream and honey, beating continuously until it is absorbed. Continue to beat until the mixture is thick enough to form gentle peaks. Spoon into individual serving glasses or a single bowl and chill in the refrigerator for 2½-3 hours.

Place the flaked almonds on a baking tray and place in the oven for 3-5 minutes until golden. Remove and allow to cool.

Serve the syllabub sprinkled with the toasted almonds and the savioardi biscuits on the side.

TARTLETS *of* DRIED FRUITS

Made with festive fruits and a honeyed custard, these delicate, reassuringly old-fashioned tarts with highly layered puff pastry sides are at once light and sinful.

SERVES 4

1tbsp raisins
1tbsp sultanas
1tbsp currants
1tbsp mixed peel
2tsp sugar
½tsp ground allspice, plus a little as sprinkling
1 size 2 egg
325ml • 11fl oz double cream
1½tsp orange blossom honey
2 x 30x20cm/12x8in sheets ready-made puff pastry (about 250g • 8oz)

Place the raisins, sultanas, currants, mixed peel, sugar and ¼ teaspoon of the allspice in a bowl. Cover with warm water then leave for 30-40 minutes until the dried fruits are re-hydrated and plumped up.

To make the honey custard, beat the egg then add 175ml/6fl oz of the cream, the remaining ¼ teaspoon of allspice and the honey. Set to one side.

Drain the rehydrated dried fruit in a colander and leave the fruit in the colander over a bowl.

Select four 10cm/4in tart tins and cut out circles from the puff pastry sheets using a pastry cutter about 5cm/2in wider than the tins; alternatively, use an appropriately sized upturned glass and cut around the rim with a small, sharp knife. Line the ungreased tins with the pastry circles (the high butter content of the puff pastry makes greasing unnecessary) and trim off the overhang. Hold a small, sharp knife with the blade pointing upright and facing towards your body, gently slice away the excess pastry without dragging the knife.

Refrigerate the pastry-lined tins for 20-25 minutes. Preheat the oven to 200°C/400°F/gas mark 6.

Arrange the well-drained dried fruit on the bottom of the pastry cups and pour over the honey custard to almost fill them. Sprinkle with a little allspice. Bake the tarts in the oven for 25-30 minutes until golden brown.

Meanwhile, whip the remainder of the double cream in a chilled bowl and place in the refrigerator until needed.

Remove the cooked tarts from the oven and allow to cool for 2-3 minutes. To serve, place each tart on a dinner plate, sprinkle with allspice and spoon a portion of cream to one side.

The Owl and the Pussy Cat

"The Owl and the Pussy-Cat went to sea
In a beautiful pea-green boat
They took some honey, and plenty of money,
Wrapped up in a five-pound note."

NONSENSE SONGS, EDWARD LEAR 1812–88

Desserts

Greek Honeyed Figs *with* Rich Yoghurt

There can be no better way of serving fresh figs than simply prepared with honey and Greek-style yoghurt. These are opened out, briefly baked and served on delicate squares of crispened filo. The fresher the figs, the better.

SERVES 4

8 fresh figs with stems
2 cinnamon sticks, each broken into 4 pieces
3tbsp Greek mountain honey
2 sheets filo pastry, each cut into 4 squares about 10x8cm • 4x3in
1tsp ground cinnamon
120g • 4oz Greek-style yoghurt

Preheat the oven to 190°C/375°F/gas mark 5.

Carefully cut the figs in half from the base to just below the stem, keeping them joined at the stem. Place the figs, opened flat and skin side down, in a large ovenproof dish and arrange the cinnamon pieces around them.

Drizzle the honey over the figs and bake them in the oven for 25-30 minutes, basting the figs every 10 minutes.

Arrange the filo pastry squares in one layer on a baking sheet. Remove the baked figs from the oven. Place the filo pastry in the oven and bake for 3-4 minutes until golden brown.

To serve, dust four plates with ground cinnamon, arrange 2 filo pastry squares on each and top each square with 1 opened out fig. Spoon a portion of yoghurt to one side.

Whisky, Honey *and* Cardamom Pudding

A classic combination, whisky and honey work well together in this comforting pudding. Although cooked in the oven, the pudding is surprisingly moist.

SERVES 4

2tbsp full cream milk
60g • 2oz salted butter, plus extra for greasing
160g • 4oz self-raising flour
1tsp ground cinnamon
4 pods of cardamom seeds
4 clove heads, the small round part attached to the stalk
90g • 3oz light muscovado sugar
5tbsp eucalyptus honey
2 size 2 eggs
4tbsp whisky
250ml • 8fl oz extra thick double cream

Syrup
2tbsp whisky
2tbsp eucalyptus honey

Preheat the oven to 175°C/350°F/gas mark 4.

Warm the milk in a small saucepan, then melt the butter in it. Allow to cool.

Sift the flour with the cinnamon into a bowl. Crush the cardamom pods and cloves using a mortar and pestle and sprinkle over the sifted flour.

In a separate bowl, mix the muscovado sugar, 4 tablespoons of the honey and the eggs until smooth then stir in the whisky and the milk and butter mixture.

Make a well in the centre of the flour with a spoon and gradually pour in the whisky and honey mixture, about 6 tablespoons at a time and whisking slowly with a fork to gently incorporate the flour. When all the flour is incorporated the mixture should have the consistency of a smooth, thick batter.

Pour the mixture into four greased 150ml/¼pt moulds or tins; do not fill to the brim as the mixture will rise during baking. Place in the oven and bake for 20-25 minutes; the puddings are cooked through when a skewer comes out clean. Remove from the oven and allow to cool.

Trim the puffed up tops slightly so that they will sit evenly and unmould them on to a casserole or baking dish trimmed side down.

Mix the syrup ingredients together and spoon over the puddings until they are saturated and leave to soak through for 1-2 hours.

When ready to serve, warm the puddings gently in a low oven for 8-10 minutes or place in a microwave on high for 1 minute, covered.

To serve, drizzle a teaspoon of honey in a swirl or zig-zag pattern on to each plate. Place a pudding on one side of each plate and a serving of cream on the other.

Making Beeswax Candles

It used to be believed that because bees left the Garden of Eden after the Fall, they were blessed by God, and it was therefore essential for candles that were used whenever the Catholic mass was celebrated to be made of beeswax. As beeswax is an expensive commodity, economic necessity now dictates that candles used in religious ceremonies need contain only 25 per cent beeswax.

The candles are traditionally made by the dipping method: melt the wax gently in a tall, narrow container and then dip the wick quickly in and out until it is coated with wax. Pull it straight and repeat the process until the candle is the required thickness. Alternatively, if you have a suitable mould, you can pour the melted wax over the wick, again taking care to ensure the wick is straight. If you want your candles to have a honeycomb texture, you can make them simply and easily by rolling bought beeswax sheets.

Whole Pears Baked
en papillote

Subtly flavoured with acacia honey and a hint of aniseed provided by star anise, these pears are individually baked whole *en papillote*, a method of neatly cooking food in its own juices. In this recipe, four rectangles of baking paper, each 45x38cm/18x15¼in, are required plus lengths of string to secure the parcels.

SERVES 4

4 pears with stems (about 200g • 7oz), peeled
4tbsp acacia honey
60g • 2oz crystallized ginger, cut into strips
4 star anise
8 cloves
1tbsp pear liqueur
120ml • 4fl oz crème fraîche

Preheat the oven to 190°C/375°F/gas mark 5. Cut 4 rectangles of baking paper 45x38cm/18x15¼in and 4 pieces of string 25cm/10in long.

Pour the honey into a shallow dish and roll each pear in the honey to coat it, then lay it in the centre of a paper rectangle. Sprinkle with the ginger and place 1 star anise and 2 cloves around the base of each pear.

Mix the remaining honey with the pear liqueur and drizzle evenly over the pears.

Bring the paper up loosely around each pear and tie at the top with the string to form a parcel. Place the parcels on a baking tray and bake for 15 minutes. Remove the parcels from the oven, untie each one in turn, turn the pear over and tie up once more. Return the pears to the oven and bake for 15-20 minutes until the pears are tender.

Place each parcel on a plate for each guest to unwrap and serve accompanied by a ramekin of crème fraîche.

Baked Custard Honeypots

Ideal for a special occasion, these velvety, smooth old-fashioned custards are made with lavender honey rather than sugar. They can be made in advance and chilled overnight, ready to serve the next day.

SERVES 4

5½tbsp lavender honey
300ml • ½pt full cream milk
200ml • 7fl oz double cream
1 vanilla pod, split in half
4 size 2 eggs, 2 whole and 2 yolks only, beaten together
150ml • 5fl oz clotted cream to serve
8 crystallized violets for decoration

Spoon 3 teaspoons of warmed honey into each of 4 150ml/¼pt ramekins or custard pots, turning them so that the bottoms and sides are coated. Place the ramekins immediately in the freezer for 30-40 minutes to set.

Preheat the oven to 175°C/350°F/gas mark 4.

Pour the milk into a saucepan, add the cream and vanilla pod and bring to the boil. Remove from the heat, add the remainder of the honey and leave to stand for a few minutes so the vanilla infuses the milk. When the milk is lukewarm, remove the vanilla pod, scraping it with a knife to ensure all the vanilla is in the mixture. Stir the beaten eggs into the milk mixing well.

Remove the ramekins from the freezer and divide the custard mixture among them. Place the ramekins in a *bain-marie* or deep baking tray and pour in cold water until it reaches halfway up the mould. Place in the oven and bake for 35-40 minutes until golden on top and an inserted skewer or sharp knife is clean when removed.

To serve, place each ramekin on an individual plate, spoon a portion of clotted cream to the side and decorate with 2 crystallized violets per person.

Desserts

Desserts

INDIVIDUAL HONEY SOUFFLÉS

Flavoured with orange blossom honey, these light, fluffy soufflés are impressively high. For the best result, use a copper bowl and a whisk to achieve the greatest volume possible from the egg whites.

SERVES 4

melted butter for greasing
90g • 3oz caster sugar
6 size 2 eggs, separated and at room temperature, 4 yolks and 6 whites only
2tbsp orange blossom honey
3tbsp orange-flavoured liqueur
pinch of salt
60g • 2oz crystallized orange rind in strips
120ml • 4fl oz extra thick double cream for serving

Preheat the oven to 200°C/400°F/gas mark 6. Grease 4 high-sided 10cm/4in soufflé dishes with melted butter and sprinkle 1 teaspoon of caster sugar into each rolling it around to evenly coat the inside.

In a large bowl, beat the 4 egg yolks with the remainder of the sugar until they are thick, creamy and pale. Continue beating and gradually drizzle in the honey in a constant stream then pour in the orange-flavoured liqueur in the same way.

Place the egg whites in a copper bowl or a very clean ceramic bowl, add a pinch of salt and whisk until stiff and forming firm peaks. Using a metal spoon, gently fold the whisked egg whites into the egg yolk mixture. Spoon the mixture immediately into the soufflé dishes. Using the point of a sharp knife, draw a circle on the surface of the mixture, about 2.5cm/1in inside the rim of each dish; this will make the soufflé rise in two tiers.

Place the dishes on the bottom shelf of the oven, making sure there is enough room for the soufflés to rise, and bake for 10-12 minutes until rich golden brown on top.

Serve immediately with a serving of extra thick double cream on the side.

Tanging

Within living memory, "tanging", or loud banging on metal objects, was thought to make a swarm of bees settle. According to the advice given in Tusser Redivivus, *published in 1744, an updated edition of Thomas Tusser's* Five Hundred Points of Good Husbandry, *originally published in 1573: "The tinkling after them with a warming pan, frying pan, kettle, is of good use to let the neighbours know you have a swarm in the air, which you claim whenever it lights." The act of tanging gave the beekeeper the right to trespass on another's land while chasing a swarm.*

Honey Packaging

There have never been many large commercial food producers in the honey business but rather individuals or small associations of beekeepers. But because or in spite of this there is a wealth of beautiful labels and packaging from the end of the last century to the present day. Generally using all the references of flowers, bees and beekeeping, the designs are often colourful, unusual and very distinctive. Today there are fewer interesting labels as more and more honey is bought from supermarkets with own-brand labelling, but search out a pot of honey from a small producer and chances are it will be as pretty as pots used to be. Country cottages, apple blossom or heather, straw skeps and rustic gates all feature strongly and somehow they always look just right.

3. *Beekeepers'* associations have always been important to the marketing of honey which is mostly produced on a small scale. Here they are selling heather honey with a picture of a bee collecting from this typically Scottish flower.

1. *The* straw bee skep appears time and time again on honey labels and advertising. It offers a safe and natural image. Interestingly this honey has been packaged and sold by a chemist so perhaps he bought in honey from local beekeepers in the area.

2. *Wonderful* artwork done for a wraparound label for a honey jar. Bees, butterflies and apple blossom join with St George and the Dragon, and strong typography, to produce a very decorative result.

4. *Make a bee-line for Be-ze-be'* seems to have been an attempt in the 1930s to up-date the image of honey. This stylish poster of the period is marketing honey as an up-to-the-minute breakfast food.

5. The bees that made this honey would have had the full range of flowers from the Pyrenees from which to gather nectar.

6. This British importer obviously felt that Californian honey was superior to home-produced varieties.

7. Australia is one of the biggest exporters of honey and has long been in the business of marketing it all over the world. This impressive label suggests a confident commerciality.

8. There is no arguing with the message on this French honey label. It is simply the best of the harvest. When this was made there was little use for weights and measures and accurate labelling.

9. This distinctive label from Boyne Valley Honey reflects the purity and food quality of honey.

CHAPTER FIVE

Cakes and Biscuits

As well as being a sweetener, honey brings its own unique tastes and savours to food. In cakes and biscuits its wonderfully subtle flavours really come into their own. Orange blossom honey in a Middle Eastern inspired layered pastry and rich dark chestnut honey in a light-as-air sponge cake are just two examples: subtle use of honey can create culinary perfection.

CAKES AND BISCUITS

Home-made cakes and biscuits, still warm from the oven, are always a treat, but only honey can impart that all-important richness, subtlety of flavour and moistness. Wild honey was the staple sweetener long before cane and root sugar, but it was never plentiful. So cakes and biscuits were a rare treat. Honey has provided sweetness, preservative qualities and moisture to an enormous range of gingerbread recipes throughout Europe since medieval times. The Polish city of Torun, on the main spice route from the East and with its thriving honey industry, became an important centre for gingerbread. And as Hansel and Gretel found out when they ventured into the woods, the sweet tang of gingerbread is impossible to resist.

A French manuscript, sixteenth century.

Apple *and* Cinnamon Cake

The aroma of baked apple and cinnamon, enhanced by a generous amount of comb honey, makes this moist, spiced upside-down cake irresistible – just right for afternoon tea, or indeed at any time of the day.

MAKES A 20CM/8IN CAKE

butter for greasing
3½tsp ground cinnamon
125g • 4oz caster sugar
2 red eating apples such as Cox's Orange Pippins, peeled, cored and thinly sliced
250g • 8oz self-raising flour
180g • 6oz butter
90g • 3oz comb honey
3 size 2 eggs, beaten and at room temperature
120ml • 4fl oz milk

Preheat the oven to 175°C/350°F/gas mark 4.

Grease a deep 20cm/8in diameter cake tin with melted butter. Mix ½ teaspoon of the cinnamon with 1 tablespoon of the sugar and sprinkle over the base of the tin. Line the base of the tin with the apple slices, overlapping them so that there are no gaps for the cake mixture to leak through. Sift the flour with the remainder of the cinnamon into a bowl. Set aside.

Cream the butter with the remainder of the sugar until the mixture is light and fluffy. Gradually pour in the honey in a constant stream, beating continuously, and then add the beaten eggs gradually; the mixture will curdle if you add them all at once. Add 2 tablespoons of flour at a time to the creamed mixture, folding with a large metal spoon then pouring in a little milk. Continue folding in, alternating the flour with the milk and finishing off with flour.

Pour the mixture into the greased cake tin and bake for 40-45 minutes, until an inserted skewer or pointed knife comes out clean. Allow to cool for 15-20 minutes then turn the cake out on to a cooling rack. The apples should be caramelized and the cake a rich golden brown.

Cakes & Biscuits

Honeycomb

MAKES ONE 30 X 19CM/12 X 7½IN SLAB

butter for greasing
3tbsp light coloured honey
180g • 6oz caster sugar
1tbsp golden syrup
1¾tsp bicarbonate of soda

Line a shallow 30 x 19cm/12 x 7½in sandwich tin with foil greased with butter.

Put the honey, sugar and golden syrup in a high-sided saucepan, and pour in 3 tablespoons of water; you will need a pan deep enough to contain the liquid when the bicarbonate of soda is added, as this will make the syrup foam and increase in volume. Place over a low heat until the sugar is fully dissolved; the sugar must be completely dissolved at this stage to prevent it from crystallizing when the syrup is brought to the boil.

Bring the syrup to the boil and then simmer until it reaches 150°C/300°F, the hard crack stage; beyond this stage the sugar syrup will burn. If you do not have a sugar thermometer, you can still test whether the syrup is ready. Using a clean teaspoon, take a little syrup and drop it into a bowl of ice-cold water. Remove the syrup and bend it. If it snaps instead of bending it has reached the hard crack stage.

Remove the saucepan immediately from the heat and stir in the bicarbonate of soda. Pour the syrup into the greased sandwich tin and leave it for about 1 hour to set. Once set, crack the "honeycomb" into pieces with the base of a knife.

Comfortingly sweet, this crunchy aerated caramel is made in a slab, rather like old-fashioned toffees were, then broken up into irregular pieces revealing its honeycomb-like structure. Good on its own, it is even more enjoyable served with rich vanilla ice-cream. Store the "honeycomb" in an airtight container in the refrigerator; air softens the candy.

Bees clustered around a honeycomb, busily producing honey in its purest form. The sophisticated hexagonal structure of the comb is unique in nature.

Turkish Delight

Authentic Turkish Delight is a delicate, exotic, rosewater-scented confection that will turn anyone trying it for the first time into an immediate addict. To make a pretty present, wrap it in cellophane, with a few rose petals if you like, and tie it up with ribbon in various shades of pink.

MAKES 25 SQUARES

165g • 5½oz very light-coloured honey
300g • 10oz sugar
1tbsp rosewater
2tbsp gelatine
2 or more drops red food colouring
60g • 2oz icing sugar
2tbsp cornflour
50g • 2oz hazelnuts
rose petals for decoration

Pour 175ml/6fl oz water into a deep-sided saucepan; when the gelatine is added later, the syrup will foam and increase in volume. Add the honey and sugar and stir over a low heat until the sugar is fully dissolved. Then bring to the boil, gently skimming off any froth with a clean metal spoon without disturbing the syrup.

Boil the syrup rapidly for about 15-20 minutes until it reaches 116°C/240°F, the soft ball stage. If you do not own a sugar thermometer you can still test whether the syrup is ready. Using a clean teaspoon, drop a little syrup into a bowl of ice-cold water and mould the syrup into a ball. If the syrup holds its shape it has reached the soft ball stage.

While the syrup is boiling, place the rosewater in a small bowl with 3 tablespoons of hot, but not boiling, water. Sprinkle the gelatine over and stir rapidly with a fork until nearly dissolved. Place the bowl of gelatine in a large bowl of boiling water to keep the gelatine liquid until needed.

When the syrup has reached the soft ball stage, remove from the heat and add the gelatine solution with 2 or more drops of food colouring to achieve the desired shade of pink.

Rinse a 19cm/7½in square or similar tin under water, to prevent sticking. Pour in the syrup and skim the top to make it perfectly clear. Leave overnight to set.

Using a sharp knife dipped in warm water, cut the Turkish Delight into 4cm/1½in squares. Mix the icing sugar and cornflour together and sprinkle over a tray. Toss the Turkish Delight squares in this and serve on a plate sprinkled with hazelnuts and decorated with rose petals.

SPICE BREAD

Spice bread, also known as *pain d'épice*, has a long tradition in many European countries where it is often moulded into a variety of shapes and elaborately decorated. Although strictly a bread, its dependence on honey and sweet spices places it firmly in the cake category. It is particularly good with a glass of Mulled Cider (page 124).

MAKES 1 LOAF OR SHAPE

350g • 11oz plain flour
400g • 14oz any dark-coloured honey
3tsp baking powder
¼tsp ground cloves
¼tsp ground cinnamon
1tsp ground ginger
1tbsp milk for glazing

Sift the flour into a heatproof bowl and make a well in the centre. Pour the honey into a small saucepan and bring it to boil, skimming off any foam with a clean metal spoon. Pour the hot honey into the flour, mixing it to form a thick, moist paste. Place the paste on greased film, wrap tightly and leave to rest at room temperature for 1-1½ hours.

Preheat the oven to 190°C/375°F/gas mark 5 40 minutes into the resting time. When this is over, unwrap the rested paste which should now feel more like a dough. Sprinkle the baking powder over a worktop and position the paste on it. Knead for 3-4 minutes until all the baking powder is mixed in. Repeat this procedure with the cloves, cinnamon and ginger then knead for a further 3-4 minutes.

Press the mixture into a greased loaf tin or gingerbread mould, or fashion it into a flattened heart shape. Bake for 20-25 minutes until it is golden brown and sounds hollow when tapped on the top; the cooking time will depend on the depth of the mould or tin, so you may need to allow an extra 5-8 minutes for the mixture to be cooked right through.

Turn off the oven and remove the spiced bread. Brush it with milk and return it to the warm oven for 3-4 minutes to set a glaze on the bread. Allow the bread to cool before serving.

Light Honey Sponge *with* Marscapone

The nutty, slightly caramel flavour of chestnut honey permeates this tall, divinely light sponge as well as its filling and topping of marscapone, a rich Italian cream cheese.

MAKES A 20CM/8IN CAKE

butter for greasing
4 size 2 eggs, at room temperature
125g • 4oz caster sugar
90g • 3oz chestnut honey
150g • 5oz self-raising flour
2tsp butter melted in 2tbsp hot water

TOPPING
500g • 1lb marscapone
2½tbsp chestnut honey

Preheat the oven to 175°C/350°F/gas mark 4. Grease a 20cm/8in diameter and 8cm/3¼in deep sponge tin with butter.

Beat the eggs and sugar until pale, fluffy and doubled in volume and the sugar is dissolved. Continue beating and slowly pour in the honey in a continuous stream.

Sift the flour twice then sift again into the egg and honey mixture. Fold in quickly with a metal spoon then fold in the butter and hot water.

Pour the mixture into the sponge tin. Bake for 20-25 minutes until the sponge is a rich golden brown and an inserted skewer or pointed knife comes out clean. Allow to cool for 5-8 minutes before turning out onto a cooling rack.

To make the topping, mix the marscapone and 2 tablespoons of chestnut honey together.

When the sponge is cool, slice it in half horizontally with a bread knife. Place the base on a serving plate and spread it with half of the marscapone mixture. Replace the top and spread with the remainder of the mixture. To decorate, drizzle the remaining honey over the top to create swirls.

Honey *and* Pecan Muffins

Freshly baked muffins conjure up comforting images of good old-fashioned home cooking and these, sweetened with acacia honey and stuffed with pecans, do not disappoint.

MAKES 6 LARGE MUFFINS

30g • 1oz melted butter, plus extra for greasing
1 size 2 egg, at room temperature
1½tbsp acacia honey
150ml • ¼pt full cream milk
125g • 4oz wholemeal self-raising flour
60g • 2oz pecans, roughly chopped
1tsp ground cinnamon

Preheat the oven to 200°C/400°F/gas mark 6. Brush a 6-mould 105ml/3½fl oz muffin tin with melted butter.

Whisk the egg with the honey then pour in the milk and melted butter and mix. Pour the mixture into a jug.

Place the wholemeal self-raising flour, pecans and cinnamon into a large bowl. Make a well in the centre and gradually pour in the egg mixture, stirring quickly with a spoon about 10-12 times only, so that the batter is not overworked; it does not matter if the mixture is slightly lumpy.

Put the batter into the muffin moulds using a large spoon and gently pushing the batter off the spoon in one movement using a spatula; any topping up would result in the muffins not rising successfully. Place in the oven and cook for 15-20 minutes until risen and golden brown and an inserted skewer or pointed knife comes out clean.

Serve the muffins hot with lashings of unsalted butter.

Almond and Pine Nut Baklava

Baklava are the traditional sweetmeats of the Middle East. Made in the same time-honoured way for centuries, they comprise wedges of filo pastry soaked in a heady honey syrup and alternated with layers of chopped, spiced exotic nuts. Although they appear complicated, they are quite straightforward to make.

MAKES 24 PIECES

90g • 3oz butter, melted
150g • 5oz flaked almonds
90g • 3oz pine nuts
90g • 3oz macadamia nuts
3tsp ground cinnamon
90g • 3oz caster sugar
20 sheets filo pastry (about 375g • 12oz)
SYRUP
250g • 9oz orange blossom honey
2tsp orange flower water

Preheat the oven to 180°C/350°F/gas mark 4. Grease a 30 x 19cm/12 x 7½in sandwich loaf tin with some of the butter.

Finely chop the almonds, pine nuts and macadamia nuts in a food processor or by hand. Mix the chopped nuts with the cinnamon and sugar.

To keep the filo moist while working, cover it with a damp, but not wet, tea towel. Cut the filo pastry sheets to fit the tin. Place one sheet of filo in the tin then brush it with the melted butter. Place another sheet in the tin and repeat the process until 5 sheets are in the tin. Spread one third of the nut mixture over the filo. Layer with 5 more sheets, brushing each with butter then spread another third of the mixture over them. Repeat with 5 more sheets and spread these with the remainder of the nut mixture. Top with 5 more layers of buttered filo.

Using a sharp pointed knife, score the top layers of filo on the diagonal about 4cm/1½in apart then again in the opposite direction to make diamond shapes. Place in the oven and bake for 45-50 minutes until golden.

Make the syrup a few minutes before the baklava have finished cooking. Pour the honey and the orange flower water into a saucepan with 4 tablespoons of water, heat for 2-3 minutes until hot and remove from the heat.

As soon as the baklava are cooked, remove them from the oven and pour the hot syrup over. Allow to cool before cutting out the diamond shapes and serving.

Buzzing Bees

"There was an old man in a tree,
Who was horribly bored by a bee;
When they said, 'Does it buzz?'
He replied, 'Yes, it does!
It's a regular brute of a bee!'"

BOOK OF NONSENSE,
EDWARD LEAR, 1812–88

Skeps

The most popular image associated with beehives is that of the traditional straw skep, one of the earliest forms of man-made hives. However, the design created problems for the beekeeper. The bees filled up the entire inside of the skep with their wax comb, so the workers were not separated in any way from the queen and her attendant drones. Thus, in order to retrieve his honey, the beekeeper had to kill his bees. The design was improved in Medieval times: a separate chamber, called an "eke", with the same diameter as the skep and about 10cm/4 inches high, was placed under the skep. The bees built a new comb in the eke, which could be easily extracted as a unit without disturbing the bees too much, particularly the all-important queen. The honey was then sliced off with a knife and the eke replaced to be used once more.

Greek Honeyed Doughnuts

MAKES 10 DOUGHNUTS

180g • 6oz plain flour
1tsp easy-bake yeast
2tsp ground cinnamon
¼tsp salt
3tbsp milk, warmed
1 size 2 egg, beaten
1 litre • 1¾pt sunflower oil for frying
50g • 2oz chopped brazil nuts
SYRUP
180g • 6oz Greek mountain honey or other clear dark honey
1 cinnamon stick
1tbsp freshly squeezed orange juice

Place the flour, yeast, cinnamon and salt in a bowl then make a well in the centre. Mix the warm milk with 6 tablespoons of warm water and pour into the well. Carefully stir the liquid with a spoon until the flour gradually falls in from the sides and is incorporated to form a smooth batter. Add the beaten egg and continue to beat until large air bubbles begin to appear then set aside.

To make the syrup, place all the ingredients in a saucepan and heat gently for 3-4 minutes until slightly syrupy. Set aside.

In a deep fryer or deep-sided saucepan, heat the oil until the temperature reaches 175-190°C/350-375°F; if you do not own a thermometer, drop in a piece of bread – if it browns the oil is ready. Gently lower a dessertspoonful of the batter into the oil, pushing it off the spoon with another spoon or spatula so the shape is nicely formed and no bits of batter go astray. Fry the doughnuts in batches of 3 or 4 until they are golden, removing them with a slotted spoon and placing them on to crumpled kitchen paper placed on top of a baking tray to drain.

Put the doughnuts in a dish with raised sides and pour over the honey syrup. Leave for 10-15 minutes then turn them and leave for another 10 minutes until the syrup is absorbed.

To serve the doughnuts, reheat them in a microwave oven set on high for 10-15 seconds or in a warm oven for 5 minutes. Serve sprinkled with the chopped brazil nuts.

Greek doughnuts, known as *loukmades*, are round, do not have a hole and are wickedly saturated with honey syrup. Although not essential, the Greek mountain honey used here gives them an authentic touch.

Afternoon Tea

"... the ample charms of a genuine Dutch country tea table, in the sumptuous time of autumn. Such heaped-up platters of cakes of various and almost indescribable kinds ... There was the doughty doughnut, the tenderer oly koek, and the crisp and crumbling cruller; sweet cakes and shortcakes, ginger cakes and honey cakes ... And then there were apple pies and peach pies and pumpkin pies; beside slices of ham and smoked beef; and moreover delectable dishes of preserved plums, and peaches, and pears, and quinces ... together with bowls of milk and cream, all mingled higgledy-piggledy ... with the motherly teapot sending up its clouds of vapor from the midst."

THE LEGEND OF SLEEPY HOLLOW,
WASHINGTON IRVING, 1783–1859

CREAMY HONEY FUDGE

Heavenly smooth and chewy, this fudge evokes memories of crinkly toffee papers, giant candy jars and childhood longings in the corner sweet shop. To achieve the right texture you will need to cook the fudge at a precise temperature, making a sugar thermometer essential.

MAKES 36 SQUARES

300g • 10oz creamy set honey
250g • 8oz caster sugar
180ml • 6fl oz single cream
45g • 1½oz butter, plus extra for greasing

Place the honey, sugar and cream in a saucepan and stir over a low heat until the sugar is completely dissolved; it is essential that the sugar does this to prevent it from crystallizing when the syrup is brought to the boil. Bring to the boil and when the temperature reaches 116°C/240°F then boil rapidly at exactly this temperature for 12-15 minutes.

Remove from the heat and add the butter. Allow to cool to 38°C/100°F then pour into a bowl and beat with a wooden spoon for about 5 minutes until the fudge is creamy and thick; this is hard work but important to obtain the correct texture.

Spoon the fudge mixture into a greased 30 x 19cm/12 x 7½in sandwich tin and leave for about 2-3 hours to set.

When set, cut the fudge into 4cm/1½in squares with a knife dipped in cold water.

Peanut Butter *and* Honey Cookies

Crisp and light, these biscuits are good served with tea or the Hot Honeyed Cardamom Milk drink on page 124.

MAKES 24-26 BISCUITS

- 125g • 4oz butter
- 60g • 2oz light brown sugar plus extra for dusting
- 125g • 4oz Australian honey
- 1 size 2 egg, at room temperature
- 125g • 4oz extra crunchy peanut butter
- 125g • 4oz self-raising flour
- 125g • 4oz plain flour

Preheat the oven to 180°C/350°F/gas mark 4. Line a baking tray with baking parchment or a baking roll.

In a large bowl, cream the butter with the sugar until light and fluffy. Slowly pour in the honey, beating continuously. Beat in the egg and peanut butter and mix well. Using a large metal spoon, fold in the self-raising and the plain flours, incorporating all the flour.

With floured hands, roll the mixture into walnut-sized balls and place on the baking sheet, spaced well apart as they will spread when baked. With a fork dipped in flour, make an impression and flatten each ball to a biscuit shape. Place in the centre of the oven and bake for 10-12 minutes, turning the tray halfway through to cook the biscuits evenly.

Remove the biscuits from the oven and carefully slide the baking parchment off the tray and onto a cooling rack to prevent the biscuits cooking any more. Allow to cool until firm and crunchy then serve.

Drinks

Throughout the centuries honey has been an essential ingredient in many drinks, from African beer and monastic liqueurs such as Benedictine, to traditional honey-whisky-lemon hot toddy.

Bee Sting

Serve this potent cocktail as a stimulating pre-dinner drink or at a party.

MAKES 600ML/1PT

2 lemons, juice only
2½tbsp orange blossom honey
100ml • 3½fl oz whisky
1 size 2 egg, white only
4 ice cubes

DECORATION
1 lemon, peel only
3½tbsp caster sugar, plus extra for sprinkling

To make the decoration, peel a long strip of skin from the lemon using a vegetable peeler and slice it lengthways to make four long, thin twists about 5mm/½in wide.

Place the caster sugar in a saucepan with 3 tablespoons of water and heat gently until the sugar is dissolved. Add the lemon twists and simmer for about 7-8 minutes. Remove the twists from the sugar syrup and lay them on baking paper. Sprinkle with caster sugar.

Place all the cocktail ingredients in a food processor. Blend until frothy and the ice cubes are crushed.

Serve in a cocktail glasses, each decorated with a lemon twist.

Hot Honeyed Cardamon Milk

Taken as a bedtime drink, especially several nights in a row, this soothing beverage should encourage uninterrupted slumber and sweet dreams. The cardamom pods are pierced to allow their aromatic flavour to infuse the milk.

MAKES 750ML/1¼PT

12 cardamom pods
1¼ tbsp clear honey
750ml • 1¼pt full cream milk

Pierce 10 of the cardamom pods with a skewer or sharp, pointed knife. Break open the 2 remaining pods, discard the skins and crush the seeds into a fine powder using a mortar and pestle.

Melt the honey in a saucepan. Add the cardamom pods and crushed seeds and stir for 1-2 minutes over a low heat.

Pour in the milk and heat gently until hot. Leave on a low heat for 8-10 minutes to allow the cardamom flavour to diffuse through the milk. Strain the milk through a fine sieve into a jug and pour into four mugs.

Mulled Cider

Sweetened with a fragrant Greek mountain honey, this gently warmed spiced cider will bring cheer to a winter's day or ring the changes at a Christmas party.

MAKES 1 LITRE/1 3/4PT

2tbsp Greek mountain honey
5cm • 2in piece cinnamon stick
6 cloves
1 whole nutmeg, grated roughly on the sides
1 curl mace
½ candied orange, peel only
1 litre • 1¾pt strong dry cider

Place the honey, cinnamon stick, cloves, nutmeg, mace and candied orange peel in a saucepan and simmer gently for 1-2 minutes to release the flavours of the spices.

Pour in the cider and warm over a low heat for 8-10 minutes but do not allow to boil.

Remove the saucepan from the heat and strain the mulled cider into four good-sized glasses. Slice the candied orange peel into four strips and place one in each glass.

HONEY, BANANA AND YOGHURT SMOOTHIE

Wholesome enough for a high-speed breakfast, this deliciously healthy drink is also a refreshing daytime energizer. Serve it sprinkled, if you wish, with bran for extra fibre.

MAKES 1 LITRE/1¾PT

2tbsp clover honey
3tbsp thick natural yoghurt
500ml • 16fl oz full cream
    or skimmed milk
2 bananas, roughly chopped
2tsp bran, optional

Place all the ingredients in a food processor and blend until smooth. Place in the freezer and chill for 30 minutes.

SPARKLING HONEY, GINGER AND WHITE WINE CUP

Made with traditional ginger beer and honey, this delectable drink is just right for a hot, sunny day.

MAKES 1 LITRE/1¾PT

450ml • ¾pt dry or medium dry white
    wine
1¼tbsp orange blossom honey, warmed
600ml • 1pt traditional ginger beer
30g • 1oz crystallized
    ginger, cut into strips
    for decoration

Mix a little of the white wine with the warmed honey in a large jug, and whisk together until the honey is dissolved.

Gradually pour in the rest of the white wine and then the ginger beer. Mix well.

Place a strip of crystallized ginger in each wine glass then fill.

HONEY EGG NOG

Sweetened by honey and fortified with brandy, this is a good, old-fashioned nourishing cold excluder as enjoyed by our ancestors.

MAKES 1 LITRE/1¾PT

4 size 2 eggs, separated
1½tbsp clear honey
800ml • 1⅓pt skimmed or whole milk
3tbsp brandy
¼tsp ground nutmeg
¼tsp ground cinnamon

Whip the egg yolks and honey until frothy and turning pale yellow.

Heat the milk in a medium-sized saucepan until bubbles are just forming round the edges of the saucepan.

Meanwhile, whisk the egg whites until frothy and just forming soft peaks. Set aside.

Pour the warmed milk and the brandy into the bowl containing the egg yolk mixture, whisking constantly until blended. Next, fold in the egg whites using a large metal spoon.

Serve immediately in mugs or thick-sided goblets, sprinkled with the ground nutmeg and cinnamon.

General Index

Italics refer to illustration captions.

A
Anne, Queen *33*, 34–5
Apicius 22

B
bears and honey 44, 83
beehives
    alvearies 10–11
    barcs 15
    bee boles and houses 12–13
    modern hives 13–15
    natural hives 10
    straw skeps 11–12, 120
    WBC hives 14, *16*, *17*
beekeeping 16–19
    tanging 104
bees
    bee society 8–9
    benefits to man 88–9
    performing bees 66
beeswax candles 101
Beeton, Mrs 96
Butler, Charles 31

C
Carr, William Broughton *16*
Charlemagne 23
chestnuts and honey 68
Cleopatra *30*, 33
Collin, Abbé 15
cosmetic uses of honey
    deep-cleansing skin treatment (recipe) 33
    geranium softening facial (recipe) 32
    hair conditioner (recipe) 28
    hand balm (recipe) 31
    history of 33–5
    honey and buttermilk cleanser (recipe) 34
    lavender tightening facial mask (recipe) 35
    oatmeal exfoliating mask (recipe) 34

D
Democritus *27*, 33
Dioscorides *28*, 31
drinks from honey 23–4
du Barry, Madame 34, *34*

E
emblems, bee 25

F
Frisch, Professor Karl Ritter von 9

H
Hartley, Dorothy 29
Herodotus 23
Hippocrates *26*, 33
history of honey
    America 24
    ancient Egyptians 20–21
    ancient Greeks 21–2
    ancient Romans 22–3
    Australia 24
    early Britain 23
    early Europe 22–3
    prehistoric 20
honey
    constituents 26
    extracting 16–19
    types 36–9
honey pots 72–3
honeymoons 55

L
Langstroth, Rev. Lorenzo Lorraine 14

M
Marguerite de Navarre *31*
Marlborough, Sarah, Duchess of 35, *35*
mead 23–4
medicinal/therapeutic uses of honey
    coughs and colds 29–30
        throat soothers (recipes) 27, 29
    earache remedy 30
    energy giver 31–3
    hangover cure (recipe) 29
    hay fever remedy 30
    morning tonic (recipe) 30
    soporific 30–31
        gentle sleep enticer (recipe) 26
    wound-healing 26–8
Mehring (inventor) 14–15

N
Napoleon 25

O
oranges and honey 65

P
Pliny the Elder *22*
Plutarch *20*
Poppea, Empress *29*, 33
pots and packaging 106–7
propolis ("beeglue") *27*, *29*, *30*

Q
quotations
    Edward Lear 98, 119
    John Milton 46
    Jonathan Swift 51
    nursery rhyme 78
    peas and honey 67
    Washington Irving 122

S
Sorel, Agnes *32*, 33–4

U
Uttley, Alison 29

Index of Recipes

(For cosmetic and medicinal recipes see General Index)

A
ale: strong honey ale 71
apples: toffeed apples with honey ice-cream 96

B
bacon: pancakes with crispy bacon 51
baklava: almond with pine nut baklava 119
beef: Cantonese shredded beef 65
beetroot: baked honey beetroot 84
biscuits: peanut butter and honey cookies 123
bread: spice bread (*paine d'épice*) 116

C
cabbage: red cabbage tossed in honey and caraway 78
cakes:
　apple and cinnamon cake 112
　light honey sponge with marscapone 118
candy: honeycomb 114
cardamom milk: hot honeyed 124
carrots: gingered honey carrots 83
cheese: honeyed ricotta with fruit crudités 49
cheesecake: lavender honey cheesecake 94
chicken:
　spicy pineapple baby chicken 63
　chicken tagine with apricots and prunes 68
cider: mulled, with Greek mountain honey 124
cocktail: bee sting cocktail 124
compôte: orange, fig and date compôte with a crunchy granola 46
confit: shallot confit 86
cookies: peanut butter and honey 123
couscous: with pistachios and currants 80
custard: baked custard honeypots 102

D
doughnuts: Greek honeyed doughnuts 121
duck: warm duck breast with Moroccan honey sauce 60

E
egg nog 125

F
figs: Greek honeyed figs with rich yoghurt 99
fish: Thai sweet and sour fish 62
see also trout
fudge: creamy honey fudge 122

G
gammon: honeyed gammon with a herb crust 61
granita: lime and honey granita 97
granola: crunchy 46

H
honeycomb (candy) 114

I
ice-cream: honey ice-cream with toffeed apples 96

L
lamb: racks of lamb with a thyme and honey glaze 67
leeks: leek terrine with honey and mustard vinaigrette 49

M
mead: old Sussex recipe 70
metheglin: Queen Elizabeth's 71
muffins: honey and pecan muffins 118

N
noodles: crunchy almond noodles 81

P
pain d'épice (spice bread) 116
pancakes: wholewheat pancakes with honey and crispy bacon 51
pears: whole bears baked *en papillote* 102
pork:
　crispy loin of pork with plum and orange sauce 64
　Indonesian satay spare ribs 62
pudding: whisky, honey and cardamom 100

R
ricotta: honeyed, with fruit crudités 49

S
shallots: shallot confit 86
soufflés: individual honey soufflés 104
soup: chilled mint and honey soup with poppadums 46
spare ribs: Indonesian satay spare ribs 62
squash: baked honeyed squash 78
stir-fry: Chinese stir-fry vegetables with honey and sesame seeds 85
syllabub: honey and madeira syllabub 97

T
tagine: tagine of chicken with apricots and prunes 68
tartlets: tartlets of dried fruits 98
terrine: leek terrine with honey and mustard vinaigrette 49
toast:
　cinnamon and honey French toast 51
　prosciutto and aubergine crostini 52
trout: smoked trout with mustard and tarragon sauce 44
Turkish Delight 115

V
vegetables: Chinese stir-fry vegetables with honey and sesame seeds 85
vinaigrette: honey and mustard vinaigrette 49

W
wine: honey, ginger and white wine cup 125

Y
yoghurt smoothie drink 125

Acknowledgements

Key: (*a*) above *(b)* below, *c* centre, *l* left, *r* right.
I B R A: International Bee Research Association
H and N H P: Heritage and Natural History Photography

Page *6 l* Roger-Viollet; *7 a* & *br* Robert Opie; *8a* M S Ashmole 1423 Bodleian Library, University of Oxford; *8b* Ron and Christine Foord; *9a* Andrew Henley/Biofotos; *10* Ann Ronan at Image Select; *11a* Mansell Collection; *11b* & *12a* H and N H P; *12b* & *13b* Ann Ronan at Image Select; *13 cl* & *cr* H and N H P; *14a* & *bl* Ann Ronan at Image Select, *14br* & *15al* Roger-Viollet; *15 ar, bl, br* & *17l* H and N H P; *19ar* Sipa/Rex Features, *19bl* Billie Love Historical Collection; *20l* C M Dixon, *20r* H and N H P, *20b* Mansell Collection; *21* C M Dixon; *22al* & *bl* e.t. archive; *23al* M S Auct F.4.15, *23bl* M S Douce 88 f.III v & *23r* Bodleian Library, University of Oxford; *24a* & *b* Ann Ronan at Image Select; *25a* & *br* Roger-Viollet, *25bl* H and N H P; *26a* & *27a* Mansell Collection, *27b* Natural Food Company; *28a* Mansell Collection; *29a* Natural Food Company, *29br* Mansell Collection; *30a* Natural Food Company, *30b, 31b* & *32a* Mansell Collection; *32l* Robert Opie; *33b* Mansell Collection; *34a* Roger-Viollet; *35ar* Robert Opie, *35 br* Mansell Collection; *36b* Philip and Karen Smith/Tony Stone Images; *43* Visual Arts Library; *44br* Robert Opie; *54* Harry Smith Horticultural Collection; *55al* Christie's Images, *55ar* C M Dixon; *55b* Christie's Images; *59* Visual Arts Library; *65bl* Christie's Images; *66a* Roger-Viollet; *66b* Alain Choisnet/Image Bank; *71* M S Bodley 264, fol. 73v Bodleian Library, University of Oxford; *72al* & *ar* I B R A; *72b, 73al, ar* & *c* Christie's Images; *73bl, br* & *cl* I B R A; *77* e.t. archive; *88-89* Ann Ronan at Image Select; *93* Visual Arts Library; *104* Ann Ronan at Image Select; *106-7* Robert Opie; *111* M S Canon, Liturg. 99. fol. 16 Bodleian Library, University of Oxford; *114b* Peter Poulides/Tony Stone Images; *120a* Ann Ronan at Image Select; *120br* Roger-Viollet.

All other photographs are the copyright of Quarto Publishing plc.

Quarto would like to thank Dr John B Free of Heritage and Natural History Photography and the following who kindly provided materials and equipment for photography: Bear Creek Woodworks, 250 Broadway, Quincy, IL 62306, U. S. A. (shelves pp.56-7 & pp.90-1); The Canadian Honey Council, 196 Stephen Street, Richmond Hill, Ontario L4C 5P1 (honey p.37); Juliet Phillips, Surrey (pp 16-19) and T R Tutton, Priors Leaze Cottage, Hambrook, Chichester, West Sussex PO18 8RQ (skep p. 120).